Search Without Fear

Search Without Fear

Ruth Hallman

Dodd, Mead & Company
New York

Copyright © 1987 by Ruth Hallman
All rights reserved
No part of this book may be reproduced in any form
without permission in writing from the publisher.
Published by Dodd, Mead & Company, Inc.,
71 Fifth Avenue, New York, N.Y. 10003
Manufactured in the United States of America

1 2 3 4 5 6 7 8 9 10

Library of Congress Cataloging-in-Publication Data

Hallman, Ruth, date
  Search without fear.

  Summary: When their grandmother dies, Dee, a high
school sophomore, goes to live with her brother, a state
trooper in Virginia, where one dangerous adventure
follows another and she begins to appreciate the
importance of the work he and his police dog do.
  1. Police, State—Fiction. 2. Police dogs—Fiction.
I. Title.
PZ7.H15469Sd 1987   [Fic]   87-12167
ISBN 0-396-08924-0

7151557

Special acknowledgment for their assistance goes to these members of the Virginia State Police:

Roger Clifton, Trooper, Canine Unit
J.T. Flanary, Captain, Canine Unit
D.G. Hendley, K-9 Training Coordinator
J.M. Lowery, Trooper, Canine Unit
W.S. McKinney, Trooper, Canine Unit
P.D. Sleeper, Trooper-Pilot
David L. Tollett, Commander, Aviation Unit
Charles L. Vaughan, Information Director

and to Robert A. Hallman, Robert E. Hallman, Lynn Hallman, Chris Harmon, Loren Nichols, and Steve Nichols.

To the Virginia State Police for their loyal and faithful performance, with special appreciation to Sergeant-Pilot E.M. Eaton and Colonel Robert L. Suthard, Superintendent

1

The blaring of the music couldn't drown out the banging on the bedroom door. Dee wanted to pretend she didn't hear the knocking. But she knew Mrs. Whitney wouldn't just go away and leave her alone. Mrs. Whitney would stand there and knock steadily until Dee opened the door.

Wearily, the teenager dropped the clothes she was holding into the open suitcase on the bed. She turned to open the door.

"Yes, Mrs. Whitney?" Dee asked the short, white-haired woman standing in the hall.

"Dee—," Mrs. Whitney began, speaking loudly. She paused. "Dear—could you—would you please turn that down a little?" She pointed to the small stereo on the table by the bed.

Dee stalked over to the table and turned off the stereo jam box. She tried to make herself calm. She couldn't be angry with the elderly lady. Mrs. Whitney had been a good neighbor to Dee and her grandmother. And Mrs. Whitney had let Dee stay with her since Gran's funeral. Dee caught her breath. She didn't want to start thinking about Gran. She turned back to the open door.

"I forgot. I won't play it that loud again, Mrs. Whitney."

The older woman smiled and looked kindly at the teenager. But Dee knew Mrs. Whitney had no understanding of the need she had for the sound of her music.

"Well—well, now, that would be nice of you, dear. Oh—and there is a telephone call for you," Mrs. Whitney said.

Dee looked down at the old patterned rug on the floor. She didn't want to talk with anyone else. She had said good-bye to all her friends. She didn't want to go through any of that again. It had been hard enough to do it once.

"Dee." Mrs. Whitney touched the girl's arm. "It's David—it's your brother calling all the way from Virginia." Mrs. Whitney sounded as if long-distance were still a new miracle to her. "Can you hurry, dear? It does cost him a good bit to call way out here to Oregon." She turned to go down the dark hall to the steps. Dee trailed behind her.

The teenager followed Mrs. Whitney downstairs and into the kitchen. Dee walked past the table to the black phone on the wall.

"Hello, David," she mumbled.

"Dee, is everything okay there?" Her brother's voice sounded very firm. Dee frowned. Ever since David had left Oregon and returned to Virginia to become a State trooper, Dee had grown more and more bothered by his commanding ways. Of course, older brothers always wanted to be boss, she knew. All of her friends with older brothers—or even sisters—complained about that.

"Yes, David, everything's just great," Dee said tensely.

"Well, do you remember everything I told you? You pick up your ticket at the airport counter. I have already set that up for you. You change planes in Chicago. And don't waste time or you might miss your connecting flight to Virginia. You'll land again in Richmond, but don't get off there. That plane comes on to Roanoke. I'll be at the airport to meet you so don't worry."

"Why would I worry? I can take care of myself," Dee said angrily. "Besides—I don't even want to come!

I can stay here. Lots of my friends have said I could live with them. Or Mrs. Whitney would let me stay with her!" She stopped a minute. Then her angry tone changed to pleading. "Please, David—I don't want to go to Virginia. I don't want to leave my friends. I know everybody here. I don't want to go to a new school. I want to stay here."

"Dee!" David broke in abruptly. "We have talked about this over and over. You don't have a choice! You have to come. You are a sophomore in high school. Who's going to let you live with them until you graduate? You can't expect any family to take on that job. I'm the one to take care of you now. When Mom and Dad were killed, Gran took us in. Now she's gone, so we look after each other. Our family has always taken care of its own. So, get on that plane tomorrow morning! And be sure you thank Mrs. Whitney for letting you stay until your six-weeks tests were over. I probably should not have left you there after Gran's funeral. I should have made you come back to Virginia with me right then." He stopped talking.

Dee didn't say a word. Tears were blinding her. She didn't trust herself to talk. Why couldn't he let her stay in Oregon? It had been her home ever since first grade. She and David had come to their grandmother's after their parents died in the car accident. Dee could remember almost nothing about Virginia. Oregon was her home. All of her friends were here! Why wouldn't David let her handle her life her own way?

"Dee—are you still there?" David asked quietly. There was no answer from his sister. "Dee!"

"Yes," the teenager finally said.

"You be on that plane tomorrow!" He softened his voice. "It's going to work, Dee. Everything's going to be okay."

"That's easy for you to say! You're not leaving everything behind you!" Dee started to argue again.

"That's enough, Dee! Enough!" her brother said angrily. "Be on that plane. And I mean it!" He hung up.

Dee slammed the receiver onto the hook. As she ran back toward the steps, Mrs. Whitney solemnly watched her. Dee refused to look at the elderly lady. She shrugged away as Mrs. Whitney reached out to pat her shoulder.

Dee raced up the steps. When she reached the bedroom, she slammed the door. Grabbing more clothes from the chest of drawers, she stuffed them into the suitcase. Turning to the small stereo on the table, she snapped it back on.

So, how was David going to like that! He probably wouldn't let her turn it on even low when he was

13

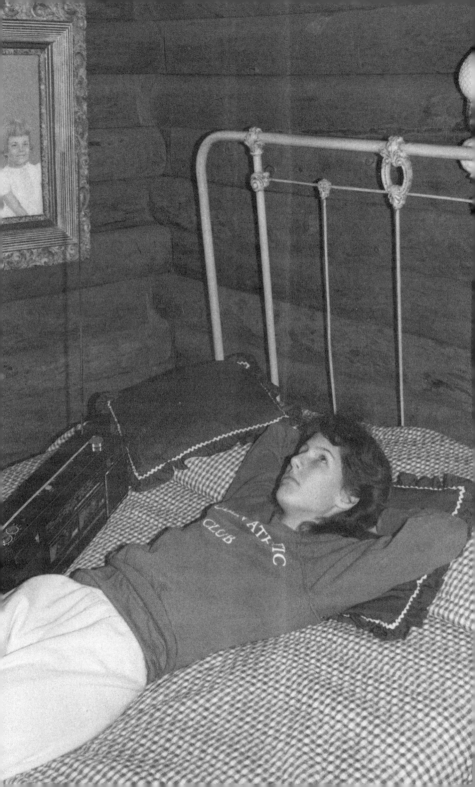

around. After all, he was twenty-six so he wouldn't like her kind of music.

Dee stretched out on the bed. She pulled the stereo jam box from the table and placed it close beside her. Everything couldn't be taken away from her!

2

Dee didn't miss the plane the next morning—but she wanted to. And as soon as the plane was in the air, she began a nervous series of trips to the rest room. On the long flight she couldn't remember how many times she waited her turn outside the small rest room. When she changed planes in Chicago, she started the pattern all over again. She grew even more tense as the plane took off from Richmond on the last leg of the trip over the mountains to Roanoke.

The 727 had been in the air only a few minutes out of Richmond when Dee decided she had to go to the rest room—again! Finally, the red lights warning the passengers to keep their seat belts fastened had been turned off. Relieved, Dee quickly stood up. As she stumbled into the aisle, she bumped her knee sharply against the outside armrest of the seat. What did one more bruise matter? Dee felt as if she had been bumped all over anyway.

Waiting her turn at the door to the tiny rest room, Dee nervously played with the gold beads on the thin chain around her neck. She pushed her dark hair back from her face. She had better try to do something with it before the plane landed in Roanoke. David would probably take one look at her and tell her to go brush her hair, or wash her face, or make some remark like an older brother.

Dee put her hand against the bulkhead to steady herself against the plane's motion. She was ready to get her feet on solid ground again. But she was getting nervous about seeing her brother. At Gran's funeral three weeks ago, she had felt she did not know him very well. They had not been together often for the past ten years.

When their parents had been killed in the car accident, she and David had been sent to live with their Grandmother Craven in Oregon. David was soon old enough to go out on his own. He came back to Virginia. And now he was making her come to Virginia, too!

The next sound Dee heard swept those thoughts right out of her mind. "All passengers please stay in your seats. Please fasten your seat belts again." The voice of a stewardess blared sharply over the plane's intercom. The red light started flashing. "Fasten seat belts."

No one moved. No one spoke. For the smallest part of a minute there was only the sound of the plane's jets whining. Then the nervous babble of the passengers' voices filled the plane. Heads started turning to find one of the stewardesses. Hands reached for one of the young ladies as she started down the aisle.

"Miss, Miss—why do we have to fasten our belts again?" The question came from one hefty passenger wedged into his seat.

"Ma'am, are we having some kind of problem?" drawled a lanky, white-haired gentleman across from Dee's seat.

"I'm sure we're in no trouble, sir! Not at all," the stewardess smoothly answered. "Possibly we are going into some slightly rough air ahead. The pilot just wants to protect you from being bumped around."

The next announcement made her words a lie. The pilot said, "This is the captain. We are returning to Richmond. We are in no difficulty. However, please return at once to your seats. Thank you."

Frantically, Dee looked at the door to the tiny rest room. The stewardess standing nearby shook her head at the teenager. Dee turned and hurried down the aisle. Stumbling again over the lady in the aisle seat, Dee scrunched against the high back of her own chair.

In a rush, the lady sitting beside Dee started to talk. "This kind of thing happened to me once before! It did! It certainly did! That time we had to fasten our seat belts and go back to Richmond, too! And the fire trucks met us and we had to get off the plane quickly!" She stared at Dee. Her eyes were blinking rapidly.

Dee nodded her head. She swallowed hard. The plane was making a wide turn. She could feel a difference in the movement.

The lady beside Dee grabbed for the teenager's arm. "There! Didn't I tell you! Feel that? It happened the same way—oh, my, oh! And that time before, the wing on the other side was on fire! I didn't see it—I didn't even know it. Everybody was just so scared no one said a word. They got us down. Then they sprayed foam all over the plane when we landed! Even when we were still rolling! We had to slide down those chutes fast—very fast! My clothes got all messed up! Oh!" she screeched. "Listen, those engines sound funny! Oh, we aren't going to make it this time! Oh—oh, my!" Her painted fingernails were digging into Dee's arm.

Dee stared down at the floor. She couldn't free her arm from the lady's frightened grasp. "Shut up—please, just shut up!" Dee whispered in a strained voice.

"What? What did you say?" the lady asked, not even aware of Dee's exact words.

From across the aisle the white-haired gentleman leaned over. He said, "Lady, your young seatmate there has told you to shut up."

"Wh—what!" The woman's face showed her shock.

The man went on in very dignified tones. "Well, this is no time for her to be forced to listen to you. In fact, I'm telling you the same thing. Close your mouth! Cease to talk!"

"Well—well," the woman sputtered. "Just how do you wish me to take that?" she asked huffily.

"Why, ma'am, take that any way you wish. The young lady asked you to be quiet. Now, why don't you do just that? And at the same time, take those silly looking red-clawed fingernails out of her arm." He stared across at the woman. His bushy white eyebrows almost met across his forehead.

The woman's face flushed a quick red. Closing her eyes, she snatched her hands back from Dee. The teenager rubbed at the red streaks left on her arm. She looked out of the window by her seat. As the plane settled lower toward the ground, fog and misting rain made a blur of even the wings. Dee could see bright flashes. She could not tell if they were lights on the wings or sudden spurts of fire. Dee felt as if she were confined in a steel tube—and she was! And she had no choice but to stay there!

Again the pilot's voice was heard over the intercom. "We are on final approach to Richmond. Please remain in your seats until you are told when to disembark. There is no cause for alarm." He clicked off the intercom.

"I don't believe that bunch of garbage," the husky man said. "This is white-knuckle time!" He fit tightly in his seat. He knew he had to worry if a quick exit was needed. Like everyone else, he was looking all around to find those exits now.

Dee already knew where the exits were. She had checked those the first time the plane's wheels had left the solid earth. Dee had read through all the emergency rules three times. If it was going to help any, she knew how you were supposed to put on your oxygen mask. She had already checked where the emergency exits were over the wings. She still hadn't figured out how to open them from the stupid diagram.

There was total silence among the passengers as the plane began dropping slowly to the runway. When the wheels screeched onto the tarmac, the pilot reversed engines to slow the speeding plane. The jet engines roared. Passengers leaned tensely forward to look out the rain-streaked windows for signs of danger.

21

There were no flames, there were no fire trucks racing along beside them. Voices began to babble in relief. At least, they were on the ground. The huge jet began to roll slowly to the far end of the runway. And *there* was the welcoming committee of fire trucks and other equipment. The jet engines whined down to a stop.

The sound of babbling voices began to rise again.

"Why aren't we going to the terminal building?"

"Why did we stop here?"

"What is wrong?"

"All passengers please remain in your seats for further instructions." That voice was different. It was not babbling. It belonged to the captain.

The huge 727 rolled to a stop near the end of the runway. Puddles of rain water shone on the tarmac like the footprints of a giant striding down the runway.

As the passengers were told to leave the plane, one of the stewardesses stood quietly by the door. She smiled stiffly and urged the passengers to have a good day as she hurried them along. Most of them just looked at her with a startled reaction. There were a few business people who seemed bored. They had been through this kind of turmoil before.

Dee struggled along in the middle of the line of passengers. The knapsack slung over her shoulder bumped the man behind her. "Excuse me!" she said.

"No problem, little lady." A slow drawl was the answer. Dee turned to smile her thanks to the tall white-haired man. He was the one who had saved her from the lady with the long red fingernails.

In the light drizzle the passengers huddled beside the plane. Dee was startled to see two Virginia State Police troopers coming toward the group. They walked briskly from the cars and trucks parked away from the plane. The troopers' blue and gray uniforms still held their rigid creases even in the fine mist blowing across the field.

The leading trooper said, "Step this way, please." Not a single passenger questioned that tone of command. The trooper led the passengers to a place away from the parked plane. They began to turn to each other with questions. One brave person fired off a question to the troopers. He got no answer. Even if he had, the next noise would have shattered the reply.

The whining clatter of a helicopter battered against them. The red, black, and white chopper swooped over a low office building near the field. Stirring up sprays of fine mist, it landed nose to nose with the big silver plane. The words printed on the side of the helicopter marked this as a further arm of the Virginia State Police.

As the blades of the chopper's rotor slowly spun down, the side door of the aircraft was opened. A trooper hopped down. He turned back to the craft and com-

manded, "Bandit, jump!" A big black Labrador dog appeared in the cabin door of the chopper and vaulted quickly from the plane.

The dog must have weighed about 100 pounds. His muscles rippled under the shiny black coat. Alertly, he stood beside his trainer who was talking with one of the other Virginia troopers.

Beside the big 727, two airport workers were quickly unloading the last of the luggage. The opened cargo doors in the body of the plane made it look as if an emergency operation had been performed on it. Another trooper was directing the placing of the suitcases in an orderly line spaced three feet apart. The luggage stretched down the tarmac.

From the crowd Dee heard that voice she remembered well. She was just glad she wasn't standing next to those dangerous red fingernails this time.

"What are they doing? My new luggage is going to get all wet! It will be ruined!" whined the lady.

"Ma'am," drawled the white-haired man, "you're going to be lucky if that luggage doesn't go up in pieces."

"What! Why would that happen?"

One of the business travelers said, "Just watch! If that dog passes by all the luggage, they will let us back on the plane. That dog will check out the inside of the plane, too. Then your luggage will be put back. We'll be on our way again. But watch out if that dog stops by one of those suitcases! If he sniffs it over good and sits to alert his trainer, then he's found something."

The screeching voice of her seatmate pierced Dee's shaky calm. "Is that dog going to search us, too? I won't let him! I don't like to make friends with strange dogs."

"Ma'am, you don't have to worry about that," the business traveler said. "These dogs don't want to make friends with you either. And he won't be searching you. He isn't trained to search people. Just watch and see if he sits in front of one of those suitcases. Then we'll see something happening!"

"Wh—what would that mean?" Dee asked this time.

"Little lady, that means there's something in that one suitcase the dog doesn't like. He doesn't like it one bit. And the troopers don't like it. And I sure don't like it!"

"A bomb!" somebody in the crowd exclaimed. "Is that why we turned around so fast and came back to Richmond? We had a bomb threat?"

"That's my guess," answered the business traveler. "That dog wasn't brought here in a Virginia State Police helicopter just to give him a nice ride, I can tell you that. He's a dog trained to search out explosives. That's what I think. I saw his kind once before at

Dulles Airport. That's a black Labrador. He's the kind the police use for sniffing out dynamite, TNT, guns—all that stuff. You just watch him go to work."

"What do you mean go to work?" the heavy passenger said grumpily. "That trooper is just playing with the dog. Look at him!" He pointed to the trooper. The officer was getting the dog excited.

"It might look that way," answered the businessman. "That's how the trooper gets his dog interested in the search. You just watch."

Like heat-seeking missiles, the passengers' glances swiveled to the trooper and his dog. They watched just in time to see the Virginia trooper give the search command to his dog.

"Bandit!" The trooper's hand moved in a signal. "Find it, Bandit!"

The big black dog began a slow walk in and out between the spaced suitcases. His handler loosely held the dog's leather leash. This allowed the trainer to keep the dog at his work. He let the black Lab check over each piece of luggage as long as he wished. The trooper didn't say anything else to his dog. He didn't have to. Bandit knew what his trainer wanted him to do.

Filled with suspense, Dee watched the dog. The other passengers watched just as closely. None of them seemed to be aware that two other Virginia troopers had walked up to stand behind the group of passengers. These troopers put their hands lightly on their holstered revolvers.

Suddenly the black Labrador stopped by a dark brown suitcase. The luggage was covered with stickers from many parts of the world. The black dog stood very still in front of the suitcase. His nose was quivering. Then the dog sat and looked up at his trainer. The Virginia trooper holding the dog's leash reached over slowly. He looked at the tag on the luggage.

"Harper, B.P.," he said clearly. "Will B.P. Harper please go with these officers? This is just routine. We want to ask a few questions."

There was no movement among the passengers. Dee turned to look around her. Other passengers were all looking around. No one moved.

"Passenger B.P. Harper, please." The dog handler's tone became a little less polite. He stared at the passengers. The other two Virginia troopers quietly unsnapped their own holsters.

The heavy, grumpy man who had earlier been wedged into his seat turned to an officer standing near him. "I'm Harper—that's me. But that isn't my suitcase! A friend at work asked me to bring it to the home office meeting." All the other passengers near him began to sidle away as if he'd suddenly developed a deadly disease. Dee watched from the edge of the group.

"That's okay, sir," the trooper said. He stepped forward quickly and put his left hand firmly under the passenger's arm. The trooper's right hand rested on his gun. He began to lead the heavyset man away from the crowd. They walked toward one of the patrol cars parked by the fire trucks.

Dee watched as a truck pulled out from the group of cars. Two men jumped from the big van. They gently lifted the stickered brown suitcase into the back. Then the men climbed into the truck again and it slowly pulled away from the area. Dee watched as the truck took the firs: exit out of the far end of the runway. She turned to the businessman.

"What are they going to do?" she asked.

"With the suitcase? They'll take it off to a spot where there aren't any people. Then they'll blow up whatever is inside. Now the pudgy guy—the passenger who says it isn't his luggage—well, he'll be questioned. I wouldn't want to be in his shoes. Those troopers don't ask you to go with them unless it's something pretty serious."

Many of the passengers in the group nodded at that. Someone said, "Yeah, you want those troopers around if you have some problem. But if you've gotten yourself in some kind of trouble, you sure don't want your name called!"

"Passenger Dee Craven—will you please come with me? Dee Craven?" A Virginia trooper stood looking over the group.

Dee stared at him. Her mouth was open in her surprise. He didn't smile but it was clear he thought he had the right person when he saw the shock on her face. He stepped toward her.

"Miss Craven?"

She couldn't speak. She could only nod.

"Will you come with me, please?" He put his hand under her elbow and led her toward another patrol car. Her knapsack banged against her shoulder. The other passengers stared after her.

3

"This way, Miss Craven." The trooper guided Dee toward one of the blue and gray patrol cars. His hand was held firmly under her arm.

"My—my other suitcase." Dee fumbled to get the words out.

"That has already been taken care of," the man answered brusquely. He turned to glance over his shoulder. Dee had no trouble guessing that he was keeping a check on the group of passengers still standing nervously with the other trooper.

"T—taken care of?" Dee asked.

"It is already in the car. Now, if you'll excuse me just a minute, I'll take you on to headquarters."

That word stunned Dee—headquarters! Why? That police dog had not sniffed at *her* luggage!

They stopped by the back door of the patrol car. Dee stood forlornly waiting for the trooper to put her in the back. Prisoners always were put in the back, she thought.

He opened the back door, took her shoulder bag and set it inside. He opened the front door and looked at Dee. When she didn't move, he shook his head, looking puzzled. Abruptly, he motioned for her to get in. She awkwardly sat down, bumping her already bruised knee on the door handle.

"Just a minute," he said. Dee thought she had gotten in the wrong seat after all, but the trooper turned and walked quickly back to the officer standing with the search dog. They talked briefly and then the trooper returned to the patrol car. Before they drove away from the area, he spoke into the mike of his service radio. "Badge 247. I have Dee Craven and I'm bringing her in. ETA is twenty minutes."

"Bringing me in!" Dee thought wildly. "I haven't done anything!" If she could just swallow. Her throat felt so dry. If she could talk, she'd tell the trooper her brother was one of THEM! That he was stationed near Roanoke and he was supposed to meet her plane there. She would tell them to please let her have one call. Please let her call her brother before they put her in jail! What did they think she had done wrong?

There was nothing in her luggage. She had her

clothes, a hair dryer, a curling brush. Her luggage had been checked when she got on that first plane in Oregon. Maybe it was something she had said. Dee had heard people on planes needed to be careful. They better watch what they said or carried these days. Too many things had happened to airplanes. The officials were taking no chances. But Dee could not think of anything she had said or done that was wrong.

Dee scrunched down in the seat, her hands clenched between her knees. The trooper drove out onto the busy expressway leading from the airport. Dee didn't want to even look at other cars moving beside them. The people in those cars would think she was a criminal. And she was suspected of something! Why else would the trooper be carrying her to *headquarters*?

Dee couldn't get the faintest squawk out of her voice to ask any questions. The officer gave all his attention to driving. His eyes roved over all the traffic. Any other time Dee might have laughed at the way cars suddenly slowed down when the drivers saw a trooper's patrol car right behind or beside them. Dee could have felt powerful, riding in this patrol car and seeing the looks from other drivers. But she didn't feel powerful in the least. She was scared.

After several miles the officer turned the blue and gray car into a curving driveway. They passed a red brick building. Flying at the tops of two flagpoles were the American and Virginia flags. The trooper turned the car into a parking lot. He got out, taking Dee's shoulder bag from the back seat. Then he came around and opened the door for her. Hoping her legs would not fold under her, Dee got out. At the officer's motion, Dee started ahead of him toward the main building.

Walking beside her, the trooper said, "He told me to bring you to the main building."

"He—he—who?" Dee stuttered. What did he mean?

Dee and the officer walking beside her stepped from between parked cars. A trooper standing in front of the building suddenly saw them. Waving, he began a quick walk toward them.

"Dee! Pete! Hey, thanks for getting Dee. That saved me a lot of trouble!" he called out to Dee's escort.

Dee found it hard to recognize the trooper from that distance. But she did know it was her brother's voice. She stopped right where she was. The officer with her kept walking. Handing Dee's bag to her brother, the officer turned to the teenager. At last he said something to her. "Hope you like living in Virginia, Dee. You certainly had an exciting welcome!"

She stared at him. "My brother! You were just bringing me to him!"

The officer looked at her. "You didn't know he was here—for training? I thought you knew. Hey, I didn't mean to scare you!"

Dee stood on the sidewalk and surprised both men by breaking into tears. She had been scared of crashing! She had thought she was under arrest! She was tired—and she had to go to the rest room!

Quickly, David reached her. He stooped over to look at her face. "Hey, Dee, what's the matter?" He started to put his arm around her. Angrily, she shrugged away. "What's wrong?" he asked again with a puzzled look.

She finally got the words out. "Where's a rest room—quick!"

"Oh—uh—this way." He took her arm and hurried her toward the building. They didn't say a word as he rushed her down the hall. As she raced through the door marked "Women," he waited by the water fountain.

Even with that emergency taken care of, Dee stayed in the rest room. Inside the little stall she leaned against the cool gray metal. She cried. She rubbed her hands over her eyes and cried some more.

She had been scared the whole way from Oregon. At first, she was just afraid about having to leave home. She didn't want to go live in a new place. She'd have to make new friends. She would have to get used to new teachers. And she no longer had Grandmother Craven for her family. She had only David. Okay, so he was her brother. When she was little, he had been the world to her. Now he seemed like a stranger. What was worse, he was going to be telling her what to do. After all the do's and don't's from her grandmother, she didn't need any more advice. She was sixteen. She could take care of herself.

Besides, David couldn't want her living with him. He had his own life. He was twenty-six! He wasn't going to like her being around all the time. She was just going to be in his way. And, more than likely, he was going to get in her way. So the tears started again.

Suddenly the door swung open. A woman's voice called out, "Is a Dee Craven still in here?"

Dee froze. Who was that? She slipped back the latch on the half-door. She peeped around the edge of the little stall. There stood a trooper—a lady trooper—surveying the row of stalls. When she saw Dee poking her head around the door, she said, "Oh, good! There you are. You *are* Dee, aren't you?"

The teenager nodded, awed by the sight of the lady in the crisp, slate blue and gray uniform. The trooper's curly hair was cut short in an appealing off-the-face style. The silver trooper's badge shone on the left pocket of her shirt.

"Hey, your brother got worried about you staying in here so long. He had to recruit me to check on you. Are you okay?" she asked kindly.

Gruffly, Dee said, "I'm fine . . . thank you."

"Okay, so I'll tell him you'll be out in a minute."

"I'll be out as soon as I'm ready," Dee said crossly.

Some of the friendliness left the eyes of the trooper. It was easy to see she didn't like the way Dee had answered. Well, I can't help it, Dee thought. Everybody was already trying to tell her what to do. Even how long she could stay in the rest room. If she had to start a new life here, then she was going to do it her way! David was her brother—not her father.

Slamming back the door of the little stall, Dee stalked over to the basins. The sight in the mirror made her cringe. Her face was puffy and red. The eye makeup which wasn't supposed to run had gone all smeary. Maybe she'd put it on all wrong. She had only started wearing it after—after Grandmother died.

When she looked at her hair, Dee stared. It was like hearing Grandmother all over again. "Cut your bangs, Dee. They are too long." So Dee had *not* cut her bangs. And now it was too late. Her grandmother was gone, and Dee wished she had cut the bangs. And she wished she was back in Oregon. And she was afraid to go out and let David see what a mess he had coming to barge in on his life. How could he possibly want her around? And why—why hadn't he let her stay in Oregon!

Dee stubbornly took another fifteen minutes to get herself looking as she wanted. Even with all the cold water she splashed on her face, it was still a little spotty and red from crying so much. She put on enough makeup to hide this from David, she hoped.

Finally, she walked out of the rest room. Her brother stared so hard at her face, she thought she must look strange. She was right about that. She had enough makeup to cover two crying jags. David finally looked away. There was no smile on his face.

"I have my car ready and your luggage is already in it. Let's get going. I was supposed to leave two hours ago," he said.

"Well, why didn't you?" she asked.

"Because of you," he said.

"But I was going to land in Roanoke, not Richmond," Dee said.

"I'd already had to change my plans to meet you in Roanoke. We had a delay in starting the training class here. I had already called someone else in Roanoke to meet you. Then when they pulled the detector dog from the training class, I heard about the bomb threat on the plane taking off for Roanoke. I knew that had to be your plane. I was just getting ready to go out to the airport but Pete said he had to be there anyway. He said he'd pick you up. I think he thought I'd better not be there if something really went wrong with the plane you were on. He probably didn't talk much to you. He's that way, but he's really a great person."

"You couldn't tell it by me!" Dee scowled.

"Hey, you're some grouch. What's the problem? Do

you need some food or something?" David asked.

"I don't need anything!" Dee snapped.

"Suit yourself," David answered tensely. They reached his patrol car parked by the curb.

Dee reached for the handle on the passenger's side. A roaring snarl exploded from the back of the car. A large German shepherd dog would have bitten through the glass window if he could have.

"Hold on," David warned her. He gave a firm command to the dog. "Easy, General—easy!" He turned to look at Dee. "That's the dog assigned to me. Nobody touches this car or me when he doesn't know them. He doesn't like strangers."

Dee stepped back from the car door quickly. "Stranger—that's me," she thought. She blinked back new tears very quickly.

Opening the door, David commanded his dog, "Hup, General." The dog obediently hopped out of the car. He sat, looking alertly at his trainer. At David's command, the dog made a quick trip to the bushes. Then he jumped into the back seat when David said, "Load!"

Cautiously, Dee slipped into the front seat. While David came around to the driver's side, Dee didn't move. She felt as if the dog would pounce if she even breathed. The hair on her neck felt electrified.

When David got in, he warned her. "Don't put your arm up on the back of the seat. Once another officer

slid his arm up to rest it and General bit him. He thought the other trooper was going to do something to me. He really looks after me, don't you, General?" He turned to look at his canine buddy. "He'll get to be your protector, too. First he has to learn you are family. Just take it easy around him until he knows you're not a stranger."

"But I am a stranger," Dee thought, "to your dog, to you, to Virginia." She stared out the window of the patrol car. The driver of the car next to her was looking at David in his uniform. He glanced at the dog sitting alertly on the backseat. He stared at Dee. "No, Mister," she said silently. "I'm not a prisoner. Not exactly. I'm just a stranger."

4

General became Dee's first friend. With him she didn't feel like a stranger. This surprised her. At first, she was afraid of the dog. Getting to know General was the best thing that happened to Dee.

After Dee and David drove to the small mountain town where he lived, he helped her carry her things into the house. Then he took her outside to show her General's kennel. It was big. A dog of General's size would not feel cramped in it.

In the next few days David taught the dog to accept Dee as one of his caretakers. Her brother made Dee learn how to take care of the dog. The first thing he had her do was to clean General's kennel and outdoor run.

"Why can't he stay in the house?" Dee asked. She

was beginning to feel secure with General. She didn't feel at ease with David—or at the new school where she had just started.

David answered her question. "General is not a household pet. He's a working dog. The state gives him the best of care. Besides, he's happiest when he's doing his job—searching or, if necessary, attacking. He doesn't like being slobbered over by human beings. So his kennel, his patrol car, or in the field on a job— that's his world. And don't you try to change that. You'd ruin things for General—and for me," David said firmly.

Dee wished her brother understood her as well as he did his dog. Maybe it would have helped her through those first weeks at the new school. But that was okay. She didn't want any advice from David or anybody else! She didn't want her brother telling her what to do, to wear, to say. Because it would have been all wrong. Everything was so different here—the clothes the teenagers wore, the slang words they used, even the things they did for fun

Some teachers had asked how things were going. She had talked with some other students in class and the cafeteria. But she hadn't made any real friends yet. Dee almost felt as if she'd entered another galaxy, that she was a subhuman being from another planet and would never be really accepted.

At the end of three weeks that changed. A boy in her study hall started looking at her, she could tell. Of course, that wasn't hard to know as he didn't try to hide his stares. Wednesday he strolled behind her down the hall. Just before she slipped into the rest room, he tapped her on the shoulder. "Hey, what's your name, pretty new girl?"

"Uh—Dee—Dee Craven," she said, catching her breath.

"So—Dee. Did you just move here?" The boy brushed his fingers through his thick black hair.

"Yes. I'm from Oregon. I came three weeks ago."

"So, Dee—new girl—how would you like to go to the dance Friday night?"

"Dance? Uh, wh—where is it going to be?" Dee stuttered.

"Here at the school. It's what they call the Spring Fiesta dance." He grinned. "What's the matter? Are you afraid you won't be safe if it's not here in this babycrib of a place?"

Dee quickly said, "Oh, no! I didn't mean that! And, yes, I'd—I'd like to go to the dance." He didn't know she would have gone if it had been in a mountain cave! You can sit home and watch television just so much. Dee was tired of being by herself. Her brother was out a lot of nights on duty or on special calls with General.

44

"Good enough, new girl," the boy drawled. "So give me your phone number. I'll give you a call about the time. You can tell me then how to get to your place." He started to turn away.

"Wait," Dee called. "I—what is your name? I don't know it."

The dark-haired boy slowly turned back. "Will— Will Snipes—a name not to forget, new girl."

"Dee. My name is Dee," the girl said angrily.

Will smiled lazily. "Sure it is. Dee—Dee, the new girl on the block. See you . . . Dee." He left.

Dee wished she hadn't said yes. Maybe it wasn't such a good idea. That thought lasted only until she told David about the dance. His show of anger proved one thing to Dee. She had made the right choice to go to the dance!

David was at the kitchen counter when she came in from school. He was making a sandwich. He turned to stare at Dee.

"You're going to a dance—already? Okay, where is it? And who are you going with? A group of girls?"

"No!" Dee answered. She was getting angry at all his questions. She felt as if she'd already done something wrong. "I'm going with a boy. You might not think a boy would even ask me, but one did!"

"Dee, I didn't mean that. I just . . ." David looked down at the floor. "Do you know anything about him?

45

What's his name? I know just about everybody in this area. Or if I don't, I can quickly find out."

"I don't *want* you to find out. *I* know him. His name is Will Snipes."

That caused the major explosion. David looked at her as if she was, indeed, a subhuman from another planet. "Snipes—a Snipes! No way! You aren't going anywhere with anybody in that family! Not ever!"

Dee could hardly breathe. She was so angry so fast. "I am! You can't make me stay home. He asked me and I'm going!"

"You darn well are not! You don't know about that family. They're rotten, every one of them. And more than that, they'll get back at me through you! Just as soon as this—this Will—finds out *Dee* Craven is the sister of *David* Craven."

"Why does that matter? So we have the same last name, so what?"

"Because I'm a Virginia State trooper in this area. And because I was the arresting officer who sent one of their older sons to prison—Dalton Snipes—a name I'd like to forget. He's a loser. The whole family is trouble. I won't let you go anywhere with anybody in that family."

Dee stared at him. Her arms were loaded with books from this new school where she had to go. She had on the type of jeans the students in this new school wore. She was trying, wasn't she, to fit in here?

"Yes, I *am* going." That was all she said. She turned and went into her room, kicking the door shut with her foot. She dropped her books onto the bed in a tumbled heap. Her shoulders drooped.

From the kitchen there came a crashing noise. There was the sound of angry, muffled words. Then the outside kitchen door slammed. Dee heard David's patrol car pull quickly out onto the street. Slowly, she opened her bedroom door to look into the kitchen. David's sandwich lay splattered all over the floor along with the pieces of the broken dish.

And that was the way it was between them right up until the night of the dance. Things were a mess. They only talked when they had to. Or they argued like young brothers and sisters do. On Friday David's attitude suddenly changed. Dee became really suspicious. He must be planning to stop her at the last minute from going to the dance. He was going to be surprised, she thought!

She was the one surprised. He didn't try to stop her. He even told her he hoped she'd enjoy the dance. He didn't sound as if he thought that would be possible. Just before Will came to get her, David was outside leading General through practice attacks with the padded arm shield. Suddenly he took the dog and went off in his car. Dee didn't know where he had gone.

There was no sign of him. She just knew he wasn't around. It didn't matter—not really. It just showed he didn't care. Anyway, Dee had won. She went to the dance with Will Snipes.

And that was rotten from the beginning. When Will parked his car in front of her house, he'd tooted the horn until she finally came out. It was clear he wasn't going to come in for her. She almost didn't go out to the car. Then she thought of how there was no way she could save face in front of David if she didn't go. And staying home meant having television as her date again for a Friday night. Well, she was in this, and she'd have to make the best of it.

Things at the dance really didn't turn out too badly at first. She talked with some of the boys and girls she'd met in her classes. A couple of boys asked her to dance whenever Will wandered out to his car. When she smelled alcohol on his breath, she knew why he was going out to his car.

She would be very happy if he'd stay in his car, she decided. Dancing with somebody whose feet were beginning to stumble across the floor was no fun. And she almost had to hold her breath after the last trip he'd made to the car. By the next time he went out to sneak a drink, she wondered if she would have to hold him up.

Dee looked over at some students standing on the

side of the gym floor. Three of the boys stood together, watching the dancers. The tallest one was staring directly at her. Embarrassed at the way Will was leaning over her shoulder, she looked away from the three boys.

When she sneaked a glance back at them, almost hoping one of them would break in and dance with her, she saw the tall one lean down and say something to his buddy. That boy quickly looked up and stared at Dee and her date. He nodded.

That was it. She'd ruined herself in one short night. It was Dee's guess all the students would think she was a drunk, too, and the boys would think she was more than that if she was out with someone like this Will.

"I have to go. I want to go home," Dee said, pushing Will away from her.

"Wh—what?" he muttered, his eyes glazed. His breath in her face made her step farther back. He held himself very stiff. No chaperone at the dance would have known anything was wrong—unless they got within two feet of his face.

"Take me home—please—now!" Dee said firmly.

"New girl wants to go. Okay, who cares!" mumbled Will. He grabbed her arm and started for the door. Dee let him hold on. He might fall flat on his face and that would finish off her name, for sure, in this school.

When they got outside in the dark, Dee moved away from him. Taking deep breaths of the fresh air, Dee led the way to Will's car. No way was she going to let him drive—until she saw and remembered this car had a stick shift. And she'd never driven that kind in her life! Not in all the five months since she had gotten her license.

Angry tears filled her eyes. Well, she wasn't staying at the school and calling her brother to come get her. That would be some sight, being picked up in a patrol car! She would have to let Will drive. She could reach over and steer if she had to. She *had* to get home someway.

Will managed to get the car started and pulled slowly, and very sloppily, out of the school parking lot. Dee sat stiffly on the front seat ready at any minute to grab the steering wheel if it appeared they were heading for a ditch. And that was something Dee was afraid of. The last few miles to her brother's small house was a winding road with ditches on each side. At least it wasn't one of the roads curving around a mountain, Dee thought.

She had to tell Will where to turn onto the last road home. He couldn't make the turn sharply enough and Dee had to grab the wheel this time. She was almost sobbing. Maybe it would be better if she made him stop the car. She could walk the last few miles home.

But she didn't stop him. This road was lonely, it was dark—not many houses along the way—and then she saw the lights of a car swing into the road behind them.

Dee prayed it was somebody who lived on this road. She turned around quickly and tried to see what kind of car it was. It was not a patrol car, for sure. Its dark shape wasn't big enough. It looked like a small pickup. It was not the size of any car she'd seen on this road.

Will stared ahead in a stupor. He was swerving closer and closer to the edge of the road. Nervously, Dee put out her hands to the wheel. Before she touched it, the lights of the car behind them suddenly swung up beside them. The car was squeezing them off to the side of the road.

A voice called out from the small truck. "Hey, Stupid, stop your car. We want to talk to you."

"Huh?" Will looked stupidly over at the window of the dark car. One front wheel of his car dipped into the ditch and the car jerked to a stop.

The pickup had stopped, too. Night sounds filled the void left by the silent car engines. Little pinging sounds from cooling motors played against the whining of the wind going through the thick leaves on the trees.

Dee could hear no sound louder than her own heartbeat. It was a frightened roar in her ears. Then came the slam of a door from the pickup. Footsteps crunched on the graveled road.

The door on Will's side of the car was jerked open. Somebody reached in to yank the boy out of the driver's seat. There was the sound of scuffling feet. The door of the other car was slammed. Will had disappeared into the dark shadows of that car. He had been roughly thrown in its backseat.

Dee sucked in her breath. Her throat was so tight with fear there was only a rasping sound. She would be the next to be yanked out of the car! And then she saw the dark figure coming back to the open door on Will's side.

Dee pushed herself as far against her side of the car as she could. She reached for the handle of the door. She'd have to run! She'd climb up into the fields and hide in the long grass.

"What made you agree to go out with a creep like Will Snipes? You don't look stupid to me." The boy's voice spoke calmly.

Dee stared at the boy who had just slipped into the driver's seat. It was the tall boy who had been watching her at the dance.

Dee couldn't even answer. Her mouth opened twice but no words came. What did he want? Why was he here?

The boy stared at her in the soft glow of the car's dome light. "You know, you have the look of a scared rabbit caught in a trap. I don't blame you. Will Snipes is nobody to trust."

Dee could only stare at him, too numb to move.

"I know you live at the end of this road. I'm taking you home. Then we'll get Will and his car back to his place before he kills himself or somebody else out on these roads."

"Me—home—where I live—me home!"

Dee's words hardly made sense to her. The tall boy just looked at her, shook his head and started the car. Rocking it gently back and forth, he pulled it out of the shallow ditch. He drove on down the road, followed at a safe distance by the small pickup he'd been in.

"Why did you—how did you—who are you?" Dee's questions stumbled out.

"Sorry," the tall boy said. "I guess I expected David to tell you *something,* no matter how angry he was with you for agreeing to go out with Will Snipes. I'm Eric Kurtz. My dad is the pilot with the State Police Aviation Unit in this area. And my job for tonight was to keep an eye on you. I would have followed you home even if Will hadn't gotten drunk. If he hadn't tried one thing, he would have tried another. He likes to test every new girl who comes to school. So the order was to see that you got all the way home safely."

That didn't even make Dee angry. David had cared far more than she could have guessed. And there was no way she could pretend she'd been anything but stupid.

She looked at Eric. "I guess that pretty well ruined your fun at the dance, having to look out for somebody so stupid."

"Hey, I'm sorry I said you were stupid. I really didn't mean it. I remember how lonely it is when you first move to a new place. But you'll like it here when you get to know people, and they know you."

"That's going to take forever," Dee said forlornly.

"Naw, it isn't. That's an order I'll give myself. We'll set up something so you can meet some of our friends. Just do yourself a favor. Stay away from Will Snipes—and anybody in the Snipes family!"

"Believe me, I hope I am never near anybody named Snipes again—not ever!"

5

Eric kept his promise to Dee. He set up a party for the next Saturday out at the small lake where his family lived.

For the first time in weeks Dee was really excited about something. That morning she was upset to see heavy fog lying over the fields outside. She stared out the window. Where was any sunshine? As she watched, she saw David take General out of his kennel. He put the dog through some practice commands.

"Crawl!" The dog began creeping across the grass toward David. When General reached David, the trooper commanded him to stay by using only his hand. David moved his right hand up along the side of his face. Then he put his arm out so his palm faced the dog. General did not move.

When David came into the house from the yard after the training, he looked quickly at Dee.

"Hey, you look like Miss Gloom U.S.A. What's the matter? Isn't this supposed to be the Big Day?" he asked with real concern. He and Dee had reached a much better understanding since the awful mess with Will Snipes. They had both tried. They had talked some. They had shared more. It was taking time to bridge the years, but they were beginning to get there. And Dee knew David cared even if she still didn't think anybody twenty-six could understand her feelings.

She turned away from the window with a scowl. "Oh, David, Just look at the fog! I was hoping today would be sunny. Eric said we can go swimming. And there is a canoe—and a float. Some of the others are bringing fishing poles. It won't be much fun on a gray day like this."

"What are you talking about? This day is perfect," David said.

Dee screwed up her mouth. "Oh, David, maybe it is if you're twenty-six but it's gross if you're sixteen."

David laughed. "You *really* think twenty-six is over the hill and heading fast for the downgrade, don't you? No, I mean this fog means it's going to be a good day. As soon as the sun gets up high enough, it will burn off the fog. It will be warm and sunny, a perfect day for the lake. You'll see."

"Really, you're not kidding me?" Dee was excited again.

"You bet! And I think I just heard a car stop outside. Is somebody coming to get you or do you want me to take you out to the lake?"

"No, Eric said he would come for me," Dee answered. She grabbed her swimsuit and towel.

"Oh, ho! Eric's coming for you, hmm?" David said with a smile.

"Don't get the wrong idea, David," Dee said quickly. "He's just being nice. We're just friends. And you *made* him look after me at the dance. Besides—he's a senior! I'm just a sophomore."

"You sure are explaining a lot. I'd say you better be quiet because here he is at the door now," David said softly as he turned to open the screen door. "Hi, Eric. Come on in. Do you have time for a coke or something?"

Stepping inside, Eric gave David a quick handshake. "Not this time, thanks. We're expecting a bunch of people out today. Mom said not to leave her to do all the welcoming. She doesn't know some of the friends I've invited." He turned to Dee. "Are you ready? Do you have everything you need?"

She held up her things. "I think I have it all. Do I need . . . ?" The ringing of the phone interrupted.

David reached over the kitchen counter and lifted the phone off the hook.

"David Craven speaking." He always sounded as if he was on duty. "Yes, she's here." He handed the phone to Dee with a questioning look on his face. She had so few phone calls any would be a surprise.

"Hello," she answered. She listened to the caller for a minute. Her face began to get pale. "No! Don't call me again! I am not going anywhere with you, Will Snipes!" She slammed the phone down. Her hand was shaking.

"Snipes!" David said angrily. "That was Will Snipes! Has he been calling here?"

Dee said, "Well, he called once. He asked me to go out with him again but I just hung up on him." Her voice trailed off.

David grabbed for the phone. "You should have let me know he called. I told you, Dee, that family would do anything to get back at me for sending Dalton Snipes to jail. I'll take care of this right now!"

"David, please don't do anything! It will just make things worse for me at school. Please, David, don't!" she begged.

David slowly put the phone down. He looked at his sister with a very worried scowl. "You just don't know that family, Dee. You just don't understand."

"But you don't understand either, David. You could make it twice as hard for me if you say anything to Will. Please don't!" Dee was begging.

"Well, I just think this creep needs to be told to leave you alone!"

She looked down at the floor. "Just—don't. Please don't call him or do anything, please!" She turned and grabbed her things up from the counter. "Eric, let's go, okay?"

The tall boy looked at David. "Will Snipes isn't in this group, David. He won't be at the lake. She'll be okay with us."

David was leaning against the counter. His hands braced him against the edge. "You're going to see to that, Eric?"

Eric understood that tone. "Yes, sir. I'll take care of it." He turned to Dee and changed the mood of the conversation. "Have you ever been fishing?"

"No—never." She looked up at him. Her eyes began to lose that frightened look. "But—yuck—do you put live worms on the line or anything like that?"

He grinned. "You'll learn to like it, believe me!"

"Never!" she laughed. As they went out the door, she called back to her brother. "I'll see you sometime, David."

"Well," he answered. "I certainly hope so."

Dee enjoyed the ride out to the small lake where

Eric's family lived. State troopers were requested to live in scattered areas from one another. This helped them cover a wider range quickly if needed.

Riding in Eric's brown pickup was her first ride in any kind of truck. His was nice but still bumpy enough to be fun.

When they turned into the gate to Eric's home, Dee had to gasp. "Oh, Eric, it's so pretty here! Who would ever guess this place was at the end of that dirt road?"

He stopped the truck right at the curve of the road. "You know," he said, "you'd think you'd get tired of seeing it and forget how it is here, but I never do. I make this turn and there it is—and I . . ."

They sat for a minute and just looked down at the lake. All the fog had gone. Just a few wisps trailed across the glass-smooth sheen of the lake. Tall white pines and green-leaved maples circled the far side of the lake. Some flowering vine twining around the fence gave off a sweet scent in the warming sun. And Dee heard more bird calls than she thought could be in one place.

Eric looked at her. "Do you like it?"

She nodded. She did not want to break the silence that belonged to this place.

Eric took his foot off the brake. He steered the car farther down the little road to the graveled parking area.

The silence around the lake very quickly turned into teenage turmoil. There was lots of it and all fun. About twenty boys and girls were swimming out from the dock. Some were dumping each other off the float, others were begging turns for the canoe. The trees on the hill surrounding the lake echoed the shouts and fun.

Dee knew a few of the students from school. She could hardly remember any of the names of the new ones she met today. Some would tell her their names, and then they'd be pushed off the float before Dee could understand. Eric's friend, Greg, finally demanded a turn with the canoe. He paddled up to offer Dee and another girl, Kelly, a ride around the lake. Shouts broke out.

"Hey, there he goes again. Old Greg is going to try to take on two girls at once. Watch out, he's a wild one!" Eric shouted.

With his canoe paddle, Greg flipped a heavy splash of water into Eric's face. Then he quickly backpaddled the canoe. He turned it away from the float and the swimmers.

The three in the canoe had gone halfway around the lake when Eric called to Greg. His voice carried easily over the water.

"Hey, Greg, Mom says there's a phone call for Dee. Bring her in, will you?"

Greg paddled the canoe quickly across the lake. He headed for the small beach right in front of the house. When the canoe bumped against the low bushes, Greg hopped out and dragged the canoe closer up onto the grass. Kelly lay back in the canoe. She turned her face up to the sun as she waited with Greg for Dee to come back.

Dee didn't race for the house. She was too afraid the phone caller had to be Will Snipes. Eric's mother would have known if it was David.

Hearing Eric's footsteps behind catching up with her, she was glad he was going to be there when she answered the phone. He reached for her arm, keeping his eyes on her face.

"Hey, Dee, don't worry. It probably isn't Will. I doubt if he even knows we're having this group out today. He wouldn't call here. And if he does, I'm going to smash his face in."

Dee tried to smile at that. She knew Eric could easily deck Will. Eric was a foot taller and he didn't have the blubber on his body that Will did. Eric was wiry in his build. And the look on his face never showed fear. He knew how to handle his world. Dee sighed. Would she ever feel that way?

They reached the house and went inside. Eric leaned against the table while Dee picked up the phone.

The voice from the other end was so loud even Eric could hear what was said.

"You don't snub me, new girl. You hear? I fixed you and Mr. Tall and all his friends—last night when nobody was awake. Just have your fun down by the lake—all of you! Have a blast!" The sound of the voice on the phone broke into a sharp laugh.

"Will Snipes!" Dee clutched the phone.

Eric whispered to her quickly. "Keep him talking! Make him tell you what he did. Somebody could get hurt because of that idiot."

Dee nodded. "Will, uh—uh." Her throat was so tight she could hardly talk.

"Will Snipes, that's me, new girl. And I told you it would be a name not to forget. So say you'll go out with me tomorrow night. Then I'll tell you exactly where my surprise is. So what time shall I come blowing my horn for you, new girl? What do you say, pretty new girl?" His voice was loud.

Dee looked at Eric. He shook his head. He mouthed the words, "Get him to tell you more." She nodded.

"What did you do, Will Snipes?" she demanded.

"Are you going with me—anywhere I say?" His rough voice grated against Dee's ear.

Dee didn't have to look at Eric again. She had her own answer. "No! I'll never go anywhere with you, Will Snipes!"

Any fun that had been in Will's voice was gone as he warned Dee. "Okay, so get this. When you and all your new friends have a blast out there today, you can thank Will Snipes!" The slam of his phone echoed over the line. Dee still held the receiver. She and Eric stared at each other.

Mrs. Kurtz came into the kitchen. "It's trouble from that Snipes boy, isn't it, son? That family is nothing but a bother for everybody. What is it this time?"

Eric was still staring at Dee but he seemed to be looking right through her. He was thinking about Will's words. "What did he say again, Dee? 'Have a blast'— is that what he said?"

She nodded. "He said it twice. 'Have a blast.' What could he mean?"

Eric didn't answer. He turned to his mother. "Where's Dad?"

His mother looked at him strangely. "Why, Eric? He's returning from an emergency call in Greene County. He has the helicopter somewhere east of Roanoke by now, I guess. Why?"

Eric didn't answer. He picked up the phone and quickly dialed a number. Two rings and it was answered.

"David!" Eric said rapidly. "Can you get over here right now? And bring General. I believe we have some real trouble."

There was the muffled sound of a question from the other end. Eric answered, "Yeah, I think it was Will Snipes. David, can you hurry?"

He hung up the phone. "Mom, get out of the house. I'm going to get everybody up on the hill and away from any buildings—the boathouse, the dock, the float, and this house. Come on, Dee, we've got to get them all away."

Dee scrambled down the hill after Eric. "What did he do? What kind of trouble could Will cause out here?"

Eric answered as they ran down the hill to the lake. "Will said to have a blast. I think that's exactly what he meant—a blast! Hey," he called out, "everybody—out of the lake! Get away from the dock and the boathouse. Go up on that open hill. And hurry, we've got some trouble!"

Eric did have a commanding way. The boys and girls threw questions at him as they splashed noisily out of the lake. But they kept moving out of the water and up the hill to the open space beyond. Eric turned to his best friend. "Greg, keep them up there. Will Snipes is taking revenge. Make them sit down low."

"Eric!" one of the girls called out. "The bugs will bite. We have on swimsuits! Or hadn't you noticed?"

He didn't even bother to answer her. He turned to go back down the hill. He stopped when he saw Dee following him. "You stay here."

"I am not. You called David. He's my brother. Besides, anything Will Snipes is doing is my fault."

Eric stood still. "No, it isn't your fault. You're just

67

one in a long row of things Will Snipes has done, believe me. But he hates your brother so he's out for you."

Eric couldn't know how that scared Dee. He didn't catch the look on her face because the sound of a siren got his attention. The blue and gray state patrol car turned into the driveway in a cloud of dust. Gravel spewed from under the tires. Before Eric and Dee reached the road, David was out with General on his leash.

Quickly, Eric told David about the call from Will Snipes. And Dee said, "Twice—Will said 'have a blast' twice, David!"

"Okay, you two. Get over behind my car. Stay low. If something blows, you'll get protection from flying stuff."

"David!" Dee gasped.

Eric was more used to following orders. Grabbing Dee's hand, he yanked her down behind the patrol car. He made her stoop so they could just see over the hood.

David turned to question Eric again. "What were Will's words? Have a blast—you and all your friends? So he knew you were all going to be here swimming. He knew you'd be out on the float and in the boathouse? What's in that boathouse, Eric?"

"Just some fishing poles and tackle, some life preservers and an old, cold drink machine, that's all," Eric called back.

David nodded. "That's where we'll search first. That seems the easiest place for him to hide something. Searching for explosives isn't General's usual work. He's trained to track people. But maybe he can show us something. Maybe a strange scent will alert him to something. We'll have to try." Turning his back to them, he began talking to his dog. "Do you want to get it, General? Want to find it? Let's get to work!" He began to get the German shepherd excited and ready for the search. "Come on, General. Let's find it!"

The dog pulled at the leash. His paws scrambled on the loose rocks. General was ready to go to work. He was excited for the search. David was dragged along as General lunged against the leash. When the trooper and his dog reached the wide opening of the boathouse, Dee and Eric could still see what was happening. David let General search in every corner. The dog nosed the life preservers. He sniffed around the base of the cold drink machine standing in the corner. The motor of the machine rumbled noisily along. When General turned away, David started to lead him out of the boathouse. As soon as the dog stepped out onto the dock, he whined. He turned to look back at the small rough building.

"What's the matter, General?" David asked. He held

the leash loosely to allow the dog to move where he wanted. Sniffing the air, General turned all around. He paced a few steps one way, a few in another. Then he pulled David back into the boathouse.

Patiently, David let the dog again go over every inch of the inside. General stopped in front of the cold drink machine. David didn't move. General stood stiffly. His nose quivered. He sniffed to the right and to the left. But he didn't stop at one place. When General turned away from the machine, David sighed. "Thought you had something, didn't you, boy? That's okay. Come on, we'll search the house."

He started to lead General out of the boathouse but again the dog stopped. He planted his feet on the rough floor and stood. Every muscle was taut and his nose lifted in the air, quivering. Then he turned back to the old machine one more time. He looked up at David, whined, and then paced restlessly in front of the machine.

David looked down at the dog. "Is this it, boy? Have you got it, General? Well, I sure can't ignore even half a hint from you. Good dog, General."

David stooped in front of the old machine. Very slowly he removed the lower panel covering the motor. And then General whined louder. He could smell better now what he had been searching for. The machine had been sucking air into the base instead of blowing it out. General had followed the faintest trace of explosive. There it sat—a crude device, timed to go with a blast at noon when all the boys and girls would be crowded around the boathouse cooking hamburgers.

After leading his dog back toward the patrol car, David praised General. The trooper called the dispatcher. He asked for the explosives team to come for the bomb. Then he turned to Eric and Dee. "Keep them at the far end of the lake until we can get this thing out of here. There's plenty of time before it's set to go off. Still, I don't want to take any chance. The explosives team should be here in thirty minutes to handle this. Then you can still enjoy your party."

Eric grinned in relief and nodded. Grabbing Dee's hand, he started back up the hill.

"Eric," Dee said, "David went down there without being afraid at all. How can he do that?"

"He's trained for that, Dee, just like my dad. Hey, troopers don't live according to average rules of behavior. They go beyond that. I've seen my dad do it enough times."

"Without fear?"

"That's right—without fear." He pulled her on up the hill.

6

"Hey, you stole my hamburger!" screamed a short, dark-haired girl. With spatula in hand, she began to chase the boy who had sneaked away with her food. She cornered him at the end of the dock. Calling for help from some of the girls, she led them in a soda-spraying attack on the thief. He finally surrendered the hamburger and jumped in the lake to wash off the sticky spray.

Eric and Dee were at one of the picnic tables close to the edge of the lake. The table was littered with empty paper plates. Only crushed potato chips and a stray pickle were left.

Eric looked down at Dee sitting beside Kelly. Dee was laughing at something the other girl had said. Everybody had just eaten hamburgers dripping with

melted cheese. Dee's hands were still messy and she was trying to rub off the stains.

"Hey, you're a mess!" Eric said to her.

Dee looked up and grinned. For the first time since leaving her friends in Oregon, Dee really felt a part of something. Thanks to Eric, she was having a super time. She'd have to do something for him sometime. He had really helped her out. It was good to feel she was finding some friends.

"Have any of you ever ridden a three-wheeler?" asked Kelly, the girl sitting beside Dee.

"A three-wheel what? Tricycle? That would fit your size!" teased Greg, sitting across the table.

"It would suit her brain, too!" Eric said.

"Come on, now," Kelly said. "I'm serious. Eric's dad has a neat three-wheeler—you know—it's about the size of a small tractor! But it's for fun—not work. Mr. Kurtz let me ride it once here, right, Eric?"

"Yeah, Kelly, but he's not here. I don't think he'd like it if I let any of you ride it. Handling that thing takes some skill. It is almost like a motorcycle. You can't just hop on it and take off."

"Don't be a pain, Eric. I know that! Your dad showed me how you have to lean in just the right direction when you're turning or you'll roll over. He said I was really good at it. Come on, let me show everybody," she begged.

Greg groaned, "Go ahead, Eric. Let her show off. If you don't let her do this, she'll find some other way to get attention!"

"Shut up!" laughed Kelly. "You're just jealous because I know how to ride this three-wheeler and you don't." She stood up from the picnic bench. "Please, Eric, just one little ride around the lake. Please!"

He scowled. "Anything to shut you up, Kelly. You're worse than a two-year-old." Pulling his keys from his pocket, he slipped a small one off the ring. "Here—do you know where we keep it?"

"Your dad showed me. It's up in that shed behind your house, right?"

"Yeah, but don't ride it too long. I don't think it has much gas in it. And remember, you can't stop it by dragging your foot so don't put your foot down on the ground when the motor is running. That's no tricycle!"

"Okay! I'll go once around the lake, no farther, I promise!" Kelly scampered up to the house and disappeared around the back. In a few minutes there came the putt-putt sound of a small motor. Kelly appeared around the corner of the house. She waved one hand at her friends.

Eric shouted at her, "Two hands, Kelly! Don't be a stupid show-off!"

Leaning back for balance, Kelly headed the three-wheeler down to the path that circled the lake. The boys and girls watched her for a minute. Then a few started a game of frisbee. Others stretched out on big towels spread on the grass by the lake. Some began to help Eric clean up the trash from the cookout.

Dee dumped the dirty paper plates into a plastic bag. She held it open for Eric while he threw in the empty soda cans.

"This has been so much fun, Eric. I really appreciate your letting me come. I'm beginning to feel not so much like the new girl . . ." She stopped talking abruptly when she realized the words she had used. Just remembering how Will Snipes kept calling her "new girl" made her shudder.

Eric saw her shiver. "Hey, forget it! Will's out of the picture now. If your brother can track down where that dynamite came from and tie it to Will, they'll get a case against him."

"Can David find out all that? Enough to stop Will?"

"Probably, so don't think about it anymore, okay? At least for awhile Will is going to be too scared to try anything. When he finds out the bomb didn't go and blow everybody away, the stupid jerk will know somebody can tell about his phone call."

"And that's me," Dee said quietly.

Eric looked down at her. "Would it help you feel any better to talk with David about this? He's still up at the house talking with Mom. After the explosives truck left, I think she offered him coffee and a hamburger."

"I thought he left with the truck."

"No, his car is still parked up by the house."

"Yes, I think I'll go up there and see him."

Eric turned to his buddy. "Clean-up duty is yours, Greg. Get everybody to work to clear this mess up."

"Yes, sir, *mi capitán,* ho!" Greg saluted and took over. "Okay, now, you slobs, you are *my* slaves now! Get to work or I'll crack my whip!"

Dee and Eric headed for the house. They walked into the kitchen where Mrs. Kurtz and David were finishing their second cups of coffee. Pushing his chair back from the table, David had stretched his legs out comfortably. The slate-blue uniform didn't give up a single crisp crease.

"Hey, you two," he said as Eric and Dee came in the door. "How is the party going now? Has it picked back up to speed?"

Eric started to answer when his mother broke in with a worried look. "Who was that on the three-wheeler, Eric? You know your dad doesn't let people ride who don't know what they're doing. He will not like your permitting those kids to use it."

"It's just Kelly, Mom. And Dad is the one who let

her start riding it in the first place. She knows what she's doing. That is, if Kelly ever knows what she's doing. She'll try anything to show off."

Through the open door came the sound of the three-wheeler's motor. Eric was right. Kelly was showing off. The putt-putt of the motor had changed to a faster roar. In full view of all the boys and girls watching down by the lake Kelly came tearing up the hill. This time she was standing up on the pedals. One hand was raised in her show of daring.

She headed across the side yard by the door to the kitchen. As her head suddenly hit the clothesline stretched across the yard, she was flipped from the three-wheeler. There was a soft thud as she hit the ground. There was a loud crunch as the three-wheeler turned over on top of her.

"Call 911!" David yelled as he ran out of the house toward the girl lying crumpled on the grass. Mrs. Kurtz reached quickly for the phone. Eric and Dee were just seconds behind David in their reaction. They ran out to the yard.

Dee had to turn away when she saw where the clothesline had sharply cut Kelly's head. Blood was flowing freely across her face. Mercifully, the girl was not conscious.

"Clean towels and sheets, quick, Eric! We have to

slow this bleeding." David yelled at the boy standing in a stupor beside him. David knelt down to the girl as Eric raced for the house. Dee stood farther back, her stomach heaving.

"What happened?"

"Is Kelly all right?"

"Where is she—oh, look at her!"

The other boys and girls had climbed the hill from the lake. They stood in a huddle away from the silent figure crumpled beside the three-wheeler.

Eric raced back to David with an armful of clean towels and sheets. Where he could, David put pressure with clean towels. Blood soaked through quickly.

"Eric," he said quietly, keeping his voice too low for the others to hear. "I want you to keep pressure right here. Just move your hand in right over mine. I'm going to my car radio to tell the dispatcher we need a helicopter here immediately."

Eric stooped beside the trooper. He looked down at Kelly's injured head. Her hair was wet with blood. The boy's face lost its healthy glow.

David jumped up and ran to the side of his parked patrol car. He reached in for the mike. He didn't try to keep anyone from hearing his words now.

"Badge 588. I need helicopter service immediately. I want priority for transfer to the Medical College of Virginia. I have a girl, sixteen or seventeen, serious head trauma. My location is Road #214 one mile off of #341 and three miles north of Ridgeland. What can you give me?"

The dispatcher answered, "I read you, Badge 588. I'm checking."

There were just moments of silence. Then the dispatcher came back. "Hospital helicopter is out on another call—I'm checking—okay, we have a State Police chopper already in the air. He's now 10-17 to your location. They are returning from a search and medical rescue. A paramedic is already on board. They're twenty minutes out from your location. You'll be on the state radio with him."

"10-4," David responded.

There was crackling on the radio. David waited to set up contact with the helicopter nearing his area. Time would be saved because the helicopter was already in the air. The expert paramedic already on board might be the difference needed to save the girl's life.

Dee stood behind Eric now. Her hands were shaking when she handed him fresh towels as the others became blood-soaked. Everyone looked up from the unconscious girl as the Ridgeland Rescue Squad car came to the scene. It was followed at a little distance by the ambulance. As the volunteer workers hopped out, David advised them.

"The ambulance to the hospital won't be fast enough.

I have a State Police helicopter on its way. Its ETA is about fifteen minutes. Do what you can until they get here."

The volunteer rescue members nodded quickly at the trooper's orders. They knew that a trooper who was first on the scene was the one in charge. Grabbing their medical supply cases, they ran over to the figure lying so still on the ground. Eric quickly stood up and got out of their way. He bumped into Dee who had been standing behind him. Without thinking, he reached for her hand and clutched it tightly. Mrs. Kurtz stood on the grass near her house. Her hand was held against her mouth.

Over the trooper's car radio squawked a voice. "Badge 588, you can now contact the helicopter directly on the TAC channel." The State Police dispatcher ended his part in setting up the contact.

"Badge 588, go ahead, 315," David said into his mike. Now he could talk directly to the helicopter pilot on the straight channel.

"315," the pilot identified himself. "Be advised we are ten minutes to your location. Do you have landing zone clear?"

"588." David replied with his badge number. "Be advised flat area between lake and barn is clear."

"315. Please advise wires or obstructions in area."

"588. House wires only going north to road. Otherwise, clear."

"315," the pilot said. "We are five minutes out to your location. Give update."

"588," David answered. "Rescue squad has arrived. Giving emergency treatment to injured. Believe this will require transfer to major head trauma center."

"315. I'll alert Medical College of Virginia our probable arrival."

Far in the distance could be heard a faint clatter from the sky. David was scanning the hills but there was no sight yet of the helicopter.

"315." The helicopter pilot spoke again. "Is this accident near Kurtz property?" The voice showed an extra tension.

"588," David said. "Advise 315 no family members involved." The trooper knew the pilot aboard the helicopter was Eric's father. He had been alerted to this emergency call as he was returning from his flight to Greene County.

"315," Trooper Kurtz called from the helicopter. "I'm approaching from northeast direction. Do you have visual contact on me?"

David started to reply, "Negative." Then swooping up over the northern hill came the black and white helicopter with its narrow red tail fuselage. David spoke into his mike. "588. I have you within sight."

"315. Advise people in area to safeguard eyes against blowing material. We're coming in for landing."

"10-4," David said. Then he turned away from the

mike. He yelled, "Everybody, heads up! Helicopter landing! Keep your eyes guarded!"

The roar of the helicopter grew to a deafening level. One of the volunteer rescue workers held a sheet over Kelly. He tried to shield her from flying grass or dust.

The helicopter settled slowly onto the ground. Blades of grass flew across the field. Some small twigs swirled up and spun away from the ground. The chopper blades did not stop spinning. Sergeant Kurtz did not leave his place in the pilot's seat. He kept the chopper ready to go as soon as the injured girl could be placed aboard. At this time he was a Virginia State trooper pilot first and a father second. He was not even looking at Eric or Mrs. Kurtz. His eyes were all for the injured girl and for the helicopter he was keeping ready for immediate takeoff.

Eric, Dee, and Mrs. Kurtz did not move. They watched as the highly trained paramedic jumped from the helicopter. He was followed by the trooper who had been out with his dog on the search and rescue. When the trooper from the canine unit saw he wouldn't be needed, he turned back to the helicopter. His hand signal to his dog was, "Stay!"

The paramedic ran across the field to Kelly's side. His orders to the volunteers were quick and curt. They followed his commands. Gently, the girl was eased onto the stretcher the volunteers brought from the helicopter. As Kelly was moved, she groaned. Her eyelids fluttered open. Her eyes were glazed, showing no awareness of what was happening.

"Oh, look at her eyes!" moaned a girl in the group of the teenagers still standing near the house.

Very gently the medical personnel eased the stretcher into the helicopter. The paramedic climbed in beside Kelly. The door was shut. Rapidly, the chopper's blades began to spin. The clattering noise increased to a deafening roar as the helicopter lifted up and straight over the hill behind the house. As the chopper disappeared over the ridge, the roar faded.

David replaced the mike in his car. Slowly, he turned and walked over to Mrs. Kurtz, patting her on the shoulder. Then he turned to Eric and Dee. He put his arms around their shoulders.

"She'll get the best care. And she'll get it fast. That's all we can do."

7

For the next few days none of the teenagers could talk of anything but Kelly. When Will Snipes did not show up at school, Dee did not even give him a thought. She knew David had turned in his report on the explosive found in the boathouse. He told her the county police were checking on where the dynamite might have come from. But Dee could only think of Kelly.

Eric called Dee every day after school to let her know the hospital report on Kelly. She was still listed as critical. No one was allowed to see her except her family.

On that first Saturday after the accident, an early morning shower spattered briefly against the windows.

Dee stood in the kitchen getting ready to broil an English muffin for breakfast. She had just placed thick slices of cheddar cheese across the bun. When the phone rang, she grabbed for it. She had forgotten her fear that it might ever be Will Snipes.

"Hi, it's Eric." The boy identified himself quickly.

"Hi," Dee said. She held her breath. She was always afraid of what he was going to tell her about Kelly. He didn't make her wait.

"It's good! She's doing much better." Eric reported. "By tomorrow they'll have her sitting up."

Dee felt tears flood her eyes. Kelly was just a new friend to Dee but she had looked so awful. Eric had felt so guilty. And Dee had felt so badly for him.

"Eric! I'm so glad! I thought she was going to . . . to . . . ."

"Die? Me, too. Nobody—*nobody* is ever going to ride that three-wheeler again. We're not even going to get it fixed. Mom says we're going to junk it. We're not even arguing with her."

"Well, is there anything we can do for Kelly? Would she like flowers—anything?" Dee asked.

"A bunch of us are fixing up a basket of gifts to take her, just small things, you know, to cheer her up. You can add something if you'd like."

"Great! I really will do anything I can," Dee said.

"Well, there is one thing you can do that would

really help. Some of us have been going over to Kelly's house. We've been taking care of her little brother, Petie. That way her mom can be at the hospital with Kelly. Today looks like a problem for us. The girl who was going to watch Petie had to go to the dentist. Maybe you could take her place?"

Dee said quickly, "I'd love to! I'd really like to help out."

"Are you sure? Petie's a real handful. He's four. Sometimes he gets out of bounds."

"That's okay. I used to stay with little kids back in Oregon. Besides, I really want to help."

"Great, that's a relief! I had him yesterday. I thought I'd have to fill in today and there's some work Dad wants me to get done around here."

"Well," Dee started to say, "David's still here right now. He's going in to see the county sheriff in just a minute. Tell me where Kelly's house is. David can take me over there on his way."

"Hey, that will be great. I'll call Kelly's mom and tell her you'll be the one coming today. And listen, Kelly's house is on the same road as mine. It's the gray one on the right about one-half mile before you reach our gate. David will know where it is."

Dee laughed. "I'm sure he will. He seems to feel it's part of his duty to know everything about everybody. I told him he was just an old busybody."

"Hmph! He may know everything—but he doesn't tell! Knowing is his business," Eric said.

"I know. I just wish he'd tell me some of what goes on. I bet it would be better than a soap opera!"

"Hey, you don't really watch those crappy things, do you?"

"Well, sometimes," Dee admitted. "Anyway, I'd better hurry. David wants to leave. And I need something to eat first."

"Eating again?" Eric teased. "Well, anyway, good luck with Petie. You may need it. In fact, you will!"

"Well, thanks so *much* for the encouragement!" Dee said with a groan.

"Listen, Mom and I are home. I'll be down by the lake cutting some of those low trees hanging over the path. But Mom will be where she can hear the phone most of the time. And Petie's not bad. He's just busy, very busy! Give us a call if you need any help. Just hang in there!"

Dee laughed. "Don't worry. I can handle it. See you." She hung up.

Grabbing her English muffin, she stuffed the food in her mouth. Then she rushed to pull on white shorts and a purple top. Her hair got only a promise, her face a quick wash. You didn't have to try to look so great for a four-year-old, Dee thought.

When David dropped Dee at the gray house, Kelly's

mother was already on the porch. She was ready to leave for the hospital. Her face showed the awful strain she had been under with her daughter's serious injury. However, the relief of Kelly's improvement was beginning to show in her eyes.

"Oh, you're Dee! Thank you for coming!" she said as the teenager came up to the porch. "There's plenty in the refrigerator for your lunch. Petie only likes peanut butter and jelly. Don't give him any candy. He gets hyper enough without it." She turned to look at the little boy standing inside the door. His face was pressed against the screen. "Petie, you be good for Dee now, please!"

"I want to go with you," the little boy sniffed.

"Petie, you know you can't yet. I'm going to take you when the doctor will let Kelly see you, okay?"

Petie nodded sadly. Dee looked at him. She quickly opened the door. She held out her hand to the little boy. "Hi, Petie, I'm Dee. Let's sit in the swing out here on the porch. I know a great story about a little boy flying to the moon."

Petie stepped out on the porch. He looked up at Dee. His blue eyes were wet. "I don't like stories."

"Oh," Dee faltered. "Well, we could play a game . . ."

"Can we play hide and seek?" Petie looked up with more interest.

Immediately, Kelly's mother turned back. She had

almost reached the car. "Petie," she said, her finger raised warningly, "no, sir, not hide and seek." She looked at Dee. "When he hides, he really hides! Don't let him start that. I don't want him to leave this yard."

"No, ma'am. I won't let him." Dee nodded firmly.

"There's a place up on the mountain behind us. I really don't want him near there. I've seen . . . well . . ." She looked at Dee and raised her eyebrows in a warning. "Just don't let him leave the yard."

"No, ma'am. I promise." Dee reached for Petie's hand. "We're going to have a good time right here, aren't we, Petie?"

The little boy looked up at her again. He nodded slowly.

"Well, I'll be back before supper," his mother said to Dee. "And I really thank you, Dee. It's very, very nice of you to help us out." She got in the car and left. Dust from the road blew up in little clouds behind her car. The early morning rain had stopped. It left only a trace of moisture, not enough to really help keep the dust down.

Dee played every kind of game with Petie that she could think of. Having been a babysitter before was a help. Still, she soon ran out of things to keep the little boy busy. Then on the back porch she found a big packing case from the family's new stove. That was great! She and Petie spent the rest of the morning turning it into a spaceship. Dee cut portholes. She taped clear plastic wrap over the portholes. Petie colored everything with his big crayons. With a smaller cardboard carton she helped Petie make a little tunnel. He liked crawling through this to get inside his spaceship. He even ate his lunch sitting snugly inside the big box.

Dee peeped through one of the portholes to find he had curled up inside. He was asleep. What a relief! She was beat. She didn't dare turn on the television. However, she did slip quietly out on the front porch to the swing. It creaked just a little when she sat down, resting her head against the high back.

Dee didn't fall asleep. She just relaxed completely. A soft wind blew across the yard. She was just daydreaming when a creaking noise came from the back of the house. Dee sat up quickly. She listened but did not hear the sound again.

Well, she'd still better be sure there was nothing wrong. Quickly she ran down the steps from the porch. She hurried around the side of the house to the back. Nothing—and nobody—was in sight.

Dee walked quickly to the back door. When she opened it, the door made the same creaking noise she had first heard. Dee swallowed hard. Somebody had gone into the house! She stood very still with her hand on the door. Somebody *must* be in the house.

Then an awful thought hit her. Somebody could have *left* the house! To be exact, Petie could have left the house! Dee didn't give a thought to who might have gone inside the house. She rushed in to check on Petie. She didn't even try to be quiet as she ran to the makeshift spaceship. Better to have him awake and busy again than to have him gone!

She looked through the porthole. There was Petie's paper plate with the crusts left from his peanut butter and jelly sandwich. His empty cup was turned over beside the plate. Petie was no longer asleep. He was gone!

Dee turned and ran out the back door. Standing by the steps, she yelled, "Petie! Where are you?" There wasn't a sound. "Petie, don't you dare hide from me!"

Dee heard a loud buzzing from a very big black and yellow bumblebee. Some crows flying over the tall pines behind the house sounded their harsh, "Caw, caw!"

Hurriedly, Dee began searching. She looked behind every bush. She checked the tool shed and the garage. There was nowhere else outside to look. Behind the tool shed Dee spotted a faint path. It led off in a direction away from the house. She started running down the path calling Petie. There was no answer.

For several minutes Dee ran until she was out of breath. She had been looking on both sides of the path. There was no sign of the little boy. Suddenly Dee stopped. The faint little path had led into a tree-shaded opening. In the middle of this was a pile of ashes and half-burned logs. Pushed over to one side were some rusting empty cans.

Dee stood looking around. "Petie!" she called softly. "Please, Petie, answer me!" The wind was whining through the tops of the trees. Birds chirped in a friendly way. But that didn't calm Dee. Her heart was thudding. This place scared her. She didn't like the way it felt.

She didn't hear anything but a funny feeling made her whirl around. No one was there. But she felt as if someone had been there. Dee raced back down the faint path to Petie's house. She had to get somebody to help her find Petie. Eric lived close. He'd come.

Running inside the house, Dee searched for the phone. She yanked it off the receiver and started to dial Eric's number. She didn't know his number! Scrambling through the kitchen shelves, she finally found the phone book on a shelf stuck between some cookbooks.

"Kurtz, Kurtz," she mumbled, her finger racing down the K's. Quickly, she dialed the number. In her mind she urged Mrs. Kurtz to answer the phone. It rang and rang. "Please, answer the phone!" Dee begged. Eight more times and Dee gave up. They *weren't* there. Eric had said they would be there! Or they couldn't hear the phone! It was too much farther down the road for her to run get them. It wasn't like the city where a neighbor could hear you yell for help.

David—maybe she could reach David! Again her fingers raced to find the sheriff's number—*if* David was still there.

"No, ma'am," was the answer from the sheriff's office. "He left awhile ago. No, I don't know where he went. You could try his home. Or I can let you talk with the sheriff if you need his help."

"N—no," Dee replied. At least, not yet. She wanted David. She hung up. Home—maybe David was home! Fingers trembling, Dee dialed her own number. There was an instant answer.

"David Craven speaking," her brother said. He never sounded off duty, even when he tried.

"David! Oh, please come over here! Petie's playing hide and seek. I don't know where he is! I can't find him!"

"Hey, slow down! Wait a minute. What happened?" David asked quickly.

"He fell asleep in his spaceship and I just went out on the porch. And he went out the back door, I think. And I can't find him! I went up this path behind his house. There was this place with old tin cans. His mother doesn't want him to go up this mountain behind their house. And Petie was really listening when his mother was telling me about this place . . ."

David interrupted, "So, he's probably been thinking about that place, right?"

"Well, he's gone—just gone!" Dee cried. "David, please! Come right now!"

"Okay, okay, just calm down. Did you look all inside the house?"

"No!" Dee answered. "But he's not inside! He's outside somewhere hiding from me. David, come now!"

"I'll be there. You just check the house. He's probably hiding in a closet or under a bed, having a ball scaring you. Go look all over the house. You'll find him, I'll bet."

"David!"

"I'm coming! I'm coming!" He hung up.

Dee searched the house. She even looked in the laundry basket under the pile of dirty clothes. Four-year-olds can scrunch up. They can hide in lots of small places but Petie was not in the house. She knew he wouldn't be.

Dee was waiting on the front steps when David got there.

"You didn't find him?"

"No—I *told* you he wasn't here!" Dee said, her voice shaking.

"Okay, okay, calm down!" David said. He turned back to his car, opened the door and called, "Come on, General. Let's get to work." The husky dog jumped out, very eager to get to work.

"Oh, I never thought about General!" Dee exclaimed. "He can find Petie, can't he?"

"We're probably not even going to need him. But this is what he and I are used to. Searching for kids. And often old people, too. Everybody in-between can usually take care of themselves. Anyway, it's my guess that child is hiding behind some bush or tree close by."

"No, he is not!" Dee said angrily. "His mother warned me about that mountain. It was as if she knew Petie would go there. And she said she'd seen something up there . . ." Dee stopped. She remembered the warning look on the mother's face.

"Saw what?" David asked.

"I . . . I don't know," Dee answered. "She must not have wanted to talk in front of Petie. Please, David, hurry! Please find him!"

"We're going to find him. Just don't worry. Listen, get me one of Petie's shirts. Don't get a clean one. Get me something that may still have the child's scent on it."

"I know! The little blanket he had with him in the spacecraft." Dee ran inside the house for the worn little blanket.

When she came back out, she saw David hooking

the long leather leash to General's collar. He was getting the dog ready for the search. "Want to find him, General? Come on! Want to get to work, boy! Come on, let's find him!" He talked excitedly. He was getting the dog worked up and interested in the search. General was pacing around and around David. Turning to Dee, her brother stuck out his hand. "Give me the blanket."

She handed him the smudged little blanket. David turned quickly back and held the soft cloth up to General's nose. The dog sniffed all over the blanket.

"This is it, General. Here's what we want!" Then he gave the command, "Find it!"

Excitedly, General put his nose to the ground. Petie had been all over the yard. General traced back and forth. David led the big dog around to the back door. Holding the blanket again for General to smell, David repeated, "Find it, General!"

With his nose low to the ground, the German shepherd lunged for the tool shed. He strained to pull David around the small building. He almost yanked the husky trooper off his feet.

"He's got it!" said David. "He's got a fresh scent. Go, General! Find it!"

The dog strained to tear up the path. David firmly held the leash. Off the restraint, the dog would have left David and Dee far behind.

Very quickly, they came to the clearing where Dee had turned back. Dee didn't feel as spooked this time. She had David *and* General with her.

The dog sniffed all around the cold ashes and half-burned logs. He poked at the empty cans. Once again David held Petie's little blanket for the dog to smell. "Find it, General," he said. He kept the dog's attention on the job to be done.

General began to sniff away from the cans. Three paths led away from the clearing. One of the paths looked as if it would head straight up the mountain. The dog sniffed all three. Then he turned around, sniffing each one. He started up one path, stopped, and came back to the clearing.

"It looks as if Petie was trying out each path," David said softly to Dee. To the dog he again commanded, "Find it, General! Let's do the job. Find it!"

The dog eagerly sniffed the ground. Choosing the path he wanted, he began to lunge up the rocky trail.

"He's got it now!" David called over his shoulder to Dee. He was keeping his eye on the rocky path. "Watch your step!"

Panting, the dog plunged ahead. Dee tried to keep up with her brother. She was breathing so hard she thought she would burst. She stopped to grab a breath. Then she saw David and General leaving her behind in these woods. They had already gone out of sight around a curve. Bushes closed in to hide them. Dee began to run, gasping. When she saw them, she felt safe again.

They came to a wide ledge. The path continued on up the mountain, but General stopped on the ledge. He began to claw his way up to a small opening in the side of the mountain. David scrambled after the dog, firmly holding onto the leash.

Dee caught up with them and waited to see what they found. Even if they left her forever, she couldn't keep up with them anymore.

General was poking his head in the opening in the side of the mountain, trying to squirm his way in. David stretched out on the ground and looked into the little cave. He was too big to follow the dog through the opening. He couldn't let go of the leash.

"Petie!" he called. There was no sound.

Dee scrambled up beside her brother. "Petie, it's Dee. Are you in there?"

Suddenly a rustling noise came to them. General did not growl. His tail began to thump against the ground. Out of the dark hole Petie's face appeared, smudged with dirt.

"I found another spaceship!" The little boy looked at Dee, his eyes gleaming.

She wanted to throttle him but he was still too far back in the hole. Coaxing him out, she said, "Come on out! Tell me all about it!" She held out her hand to him. He took it and she began to drag him out of the small cave.

He babbled excitedly, "I had to go through this part—just like the tunnel you made for me. And then there's a bigger part inside and it's all nice and has a blanket like mine and some food!"

"Petie! Get up! What made you do that?" Dee had not really listened to the little boy's words. She had him all the way out of the cave now. She made him slide back down to the ledge. David was patting General and praising him, "Good job! Good dog!"

The dog looked up at the trooper. He seemed to be saying, "Where's my reward?" David held out the towel. He always let his dog play with it at the end of a job. This tug-of-war with his trainer was always part of General's reward for his success. The dog loved nothing better.

Dee and the child started back down the path. Petie squirmed to get away. She held his hand tightly.

"I left something. I have to go back." He began to cry when they were halfway back to the house.

"What?" Dee asked crossly.

"My space helmet! It's back there. I want it!" He struggled to get free.

"Hey," David said firmly as he came right behind them. "You are coming back to the house with me."

Scooping the little boy up in one arm, he gave a command to his dog. "Heel, General." The dog promptly came to David's left side. He stayed right beside his trainer's knee. Then David turned to Dee. "Look, Dee, you run back up there. Get his space helmet. If you don't, he will probably try to go back himself sometime."

"David, I'm scared." Dee stood in the pathway.

"Aw, come on, Dee. There's nothing up there. I'll wait right here and hold him. It won't take you a second."

"Oh, all right," Dee muttered. She started slowly back up the trail. As she turned a curve in the path, she could hear David talking to Petie. He was telling the little boy never, not ever, ever to run off again.

Soon the bushes hid them from her sight. She climbed the last few feet to the ledge and scrambled up to the opening in the side of the mountain. Lying on the ground, she reached her hand inside the cave. Shivering, she felt around in the dark dirt. "Ugh—spiders and snakes! Yuck!" she said when her fingers touched something soft. Then she felt the hard, plastic helmet and quickly drew it out.

"Whew, I never want to come back up here again," she muttered. She stood up to brush off the dirt and leaves. An eerie feeling crept over her. She started to whirl around but she was grabbed from the back. A filthy hand slapped over her mouth. A denim-covered arm wrapped around her arms, pinning them against her body. She was lifted off her feet and dragged into the bushes near the cave.

From the path below she could hear General barking excitedly. David's voice drifted up to her. "What is it? What is it, General? What's the matter? Do you hear something I can't hear?"

"David!" Dee tried to scream through the dirty fingers covering her mouth. She couldn't get out a sound as she was pulled deeper and deeper into the woods.

8

Dee was being dragged backwards through the woods. She scrambled to get her feet under her but she was being jerked along too fast. She kept moaning as loudly as she could.

"Um—um," was the only sound she could make. The dirty hand tightened like a vise over her mouth. She could smell filth and sweat and tobacco-stained fingers. She still hadn't seen the face of her captor. It was a man. She knew by the size of him. As he dragged her along, she caught glimpses of dirty pants and old work shoes.

Finally, the man stopped dragging her. They had reached a small stream. The man held her tightly. When she tried to moan, he gave her a jerk.

"Shut up, girl. I don't want nobody following me. I

need to hear if somebody's on my trail. So you be quiet!"

At once, Dee was quiet. She wanted to listen, too. If she could hear David coming behind them, he'd have General! They would attack the man and get her free. Dee strained to listen just as the man holding her did. There were the sounds of many locusts humming steadily in the trees around them. Birds were constantly singing their conversations. There was no sound of feet brushing through the bushes after them. No sound of a dog's panting lunge along the trail. The only noises at all were the sounds of a forest at peace.

"Oh, somebody help me!" Dee thought. "David's far back on the other side of that hill. He has Petie with him. Even when he realizes I'm not there, he can't come after me with a four-year-old! What am I going to do?"

Panicking, she tried to squirm away from the man. He tightened his hold on her until she could hardly get a breath. His fingers over her mouth were like steel coils.

"Don't try it!" he warned in her ear. "Just don't try anything! You got so nosy—you found my place up there. I let the kid go. He didn't know nothing. But you had to come back and check around, didn't you? And you had to call in the trooper, didn't you? Well, that trooper got me once but he won't catch me again or my name ain't Dalton Snipes!"

Dee stiffened. Dalton Snipes! But he was supposed to be in prison! David was the officer who had arrested Dalton Snipes and sent him to prison. How could the man be here? Then she had another terrifying thought. Did he know who she was? Did he know she was David's sister? What would he do with her because he hated David so much?

"That's good, girl. You've gotten real nice and quiet. I ain't gonna hurt you, not 'less you get in my way or try to pull some smart trick. I got out of that jail and I ain't going back. Just you act nice. As soon as my brother can find a car to get for me, I'll be away from here. And maybe you'll be set free," he paused. "But maybe not. It might be good if I have you along for awhile, for a kind of extra protection."

Dee was almost limp. He didn't know who she was yet. Maybe he would let her go free before he found out! But he might take her when he began his run.

The man muttered in her ear, "Now, you come along easy. I'm getting tired of dragging you. My leg's hurt from climbing through that pipe out of the prison. So don't you be causing me no trouble. We got a ways to go yet. It'll be easier going if I got you tied up right. So, now don't do nothing dumb. You put your arms behind your back now, real easy."

Slowly, he loosened his hold on her arms just enough to let her slide her arms close to her body and to her back. When he began to take his hand from her mouth, she started a scream. He cut that off with his dirty hand slapped across her mouth again.

"Girl!" he said with a hissing threat, "are you going to make me hurt you? Don't be doing that, you hear! Guess I better show you what's going to stop you the next time you try anything. Anything, you hear me, girl?" And right in front of her eyes he held up a sharp knife, its blade pointed.

Dee's body stiffened as he put the knife point against her back.

"Now, you be good, girl. I don't want to hurt you but I got to get away from here. And you ain't going to stop me just 'cause you were nosing around my hiding place."

Suddenly he got very quiet. Far away the sound of barking dogs echoed in the hills. Dee became just as quiet to listen. Was it General! Was he tracking their trail with David?

Dalton Snipes snorted, "That ain't nothing but a bunch of hounds. They must of found themselves a rabbit or a fox to chase."

Dee almost cried. It wasn't General. She could tell now herself. There were several dogs barking way up on a ridge. Their baying echoed as they chased some frightened animal.

Dalton warned her once more. "Now, don't you be

forgetting my knife, you hear? I got to tie you up. I hurt too much to be dragging you along at the same time. Get your hands behind your back."

Dee had to do what he said. She did not know this man. She had no way of knowing what he would do. She didn't even know why he had been put in jail. It could have been robbery. It could have been worse— even murder. She had to keep herself calm and hope David and General would find her. "Find me before it's too late," Dee thought. "Oh, David—find me!"

Dalton Snipes had pulled some rope from his pocket. He tied her hands very tightly behind her back. The rope burned into her skin. But that was not as bad as the big filthy handkerchief he tied over her mouth. It reeked of sweat and filth. Dee gagged.

"Okay, girl, let's go. I'll not be tying your feet yet. You got some walking to do. Just keep moving where I tell you. Go along the edge of this lake but keep far enough up from the edge of the water. We're hidden this far up into the bushes. And remember, you don't try something you think's smart. I got my knife out. You hear, girl?"

Silently, Dee nodded. She thought, "Girl! Don't they know anything else to call somebody? Didn't they have any girls in their family with names?" Then she thought, "No, it will be better if he keeps calling me girl. That means he doesn't know I'm Dee, David Craven's sister."

They walked what seemed like hours to Dee. They had climbed up the hill around this lake to keep out of sight. As long as they'd been walking, Dee had seen no one. Gnats buzzed in front of her face as they hiked along. Using her shoulder, she shrugged the insects away the best she could. They bit at the back of her neck where her hair was hot and sticky against her skin.

Every now and then Dalton Snipes stopped to listen for anyone trailing them. Each time he would nod with satisfaction. Dee listened harder than he did, but she heard nothing. As he made her keep hiking along the slanted hill through the thick bushes, her head drooped forlornly.

When they came up on a barbed-wire fence, he grabbed the back of her shirt. "We're about there, girl. Just crawl between these wires. Here, get on through."

She bent over and clambered through, scratching her arms and legs against the rusty barbs. When they got on the other side, Dalton hurried her over to a shack near the stream flowing below the lake's earthen dam. She stumbled along over the rocks.

Giving her a slight push, he shoved her down onto the sagging porch. Part of the wooden wall still standing hid her from the weed-grown meadow stretching out in front of the old shack. Dee cringed at the black spiders scurrying away from the rotten wood.

"Stick out your feet, girl," Dalton Snipes said. Dee

stared at him. "Your feet! Your feet, girl, I said!" He yanked her feet straight out and getting rope from inside the old cabin, he tied her ankles tightly together. Then he stood up and looked down at her. It was the first time Dee had really seen his face. It was as dirty as the rest of him. His face had a stubbly two-day growth and around his lips were traces of food he hadn't bothered to rub off. Dee gagged again.

"Don't you go getting sick on me, girl. I ain't got time to do nothing for you. I got to get out of this county."

He turned and went into the old shack. Dee could hear cans rattling and falling. She heard the man muttering to himself, "Now, where'd I put that pepper? Here it is!"

He came back out with a big can of black pepper. Not even looking at Dee, he still talked to her. "I won't need none of these supplies now. I got to get out of here. But I don't want that trooper and his dog following my trail. I'm tracking back up the way we came. I'll sprinkle pepper all over where we was walking. That dog won't be able to smell a thing! He probably won't ever smell again after he gets enough of this pepper," he cackled. "And I got to go find Will up there somewheres. Got to see if he found me a car yet."

He started back up through the bushes, sprinkling black pepper as he went.

Dee stared after him. He was leaving! But what good

would that do? She couldn't move. Her legs were tied tight. Her hands were tied. The filthy gag was still around her mouth. Dee moved her shoulder to try to brush the tears from her eyes. The dirt from her shirt made her eyes sting. Dalton Snipes had left her sitting backed up against the door of the tumbling old shack. At least she had something to lean against even if the wood was rotting.

She started to draw her knees up on the old wood. A movement high up in the porch roof caught her eye. Curling down from the rotting rafters was a big snake. As it stretched down to the dirt below, Dee saw it must be six feet long. The black snake slithered quietly down from the sagging roof. It squirmed its way over the ground on the far side of the shed.

Dee didn't move her legs, awkwardly bent in a half-way position. "Please, oh, please," she thought. "Please be a nice snake. Don't be the biting kind." She didn't move. She hardly breathed.

The snake slithered across the dirt. It headed swiftly for a big rock near the shed. The stone was warm from the heat of the sun beating down on it all day. The snake squirmed up on the rock and curled itself around. Dee couldn't take her eyes off it. "Please be a good snake—please stay there. Don't come back over here."

Suddenly the snake dropped down into the grass just below the rock. In an instant it was completely

114

hidden from sight before Dee could even see where it went. But she knew why it had gone.

There was a rustling in the bushes by the lake. Somebody—or something—was coming this way. Then she heard voices, but not the voices she wished to hear—not David or Eric. She heard Dalton Snipes talking and she heard *Will* Snipes answer. Will Snipes who hated her now—Will Snipes who knew who she was.

Dalton was asking his brother, "So, this car you got me—did anybody see you take it?"

"Naw, I told you nobody saw me! This guy hopped out at Bacon's Store, ran in for a cold drink or something. He left the keys in the car and the motor still running. I was out of there with the car before that guy pulled the tab on his soda, I'll bet you. I hid the car on the other side of Koons' old barn, over on Route 747. And it's a cool car, Dalton! And the gas tank's almost full, too. It's a four-door but it'll really move! You can get out of the county fast in this one," Will said.

The two brothers pushed their way through the bushes and came around the corner of the shed. Dalton walked quickly on inside and started gathering his things. Will stopped in front of the shack, staring down at the girl on the rotting porch. The boy held a rifle loosely against his shoulder.

"I swear, Dalton, what's this? What have you done! What's *she* doing here?"

Dalton stepped out of the back room. "Her? She was messing around my cave up there on the mountain. Her little boy found it. She came after him with that David Craven, him and his dog. They all left. Then she came back snooping around. I couldn't let her go tell Craven what she found. I didn't want him going in that cave. He'd know where to start looking for me just as soon as them prison guards get out the word on me."

"He'd know anyway, you stupid!" Will yelled at his brother. "Dalton, do you know you're really stupid! I ain't going to help you anymore. You've gotten us in a real mess now! Do you know what you've done?"

"Hey, I ain't going to hurt her. I'll just leave her tied up here and somebody will find her soon. She don't know me. She don't know you. She can't tell on us!" he snarled.

"Yeah, well, do you know who this is? Well, you just kidnapped David Craven's sister. She knows who *both* of us are!" Will yelled.

Dalton whirled around to stare at Dee. His eyes narrowed with anger. "Craven's sister! Well, what are we going to do with her now? We can't leave her to tell on us! So what are we going to do with her?"

The Snipes brothers stared down at Dee.

116

9

Have you ever been so scared you stopped breathing? Stopped swallowing, or blinking your eyes? Dee's body was jerking in little spasms as she lay curled up on the dirty boards. The Snipes brothers had not touched her yet. They were still arguing over what to do with her.

"Dalton, now you got me in trouble, too! Why did you have to drag that girl here? She can tell that I was helping you and that I was the one stole the car for you! You've really done it this time. Now I can't stay in this county either! I'll have to get away with you!" Will yelled at his brother.

"No, you ain't! I don't want no teenager kid tagging along with me. I'm going to Texas, maybe even Mexico! You ain't going to mess things up for me. You stay here—or go where you want to—but you ain't coming with me!" Dalton turned and spit out tobacco juice onto the ground.

"Well, I got the car for you, didn't I?" Will angrily asked his older brother.

"That don't make no difference if you did. You ain't going with me and get in my way," Dalton answered.

"Well, they'll know all about what I did to help you," Will said, his voice shaking. "This whole county will know. She'll tell." Will pointed at Dee, his hand shaking.

"Well, you know how to take care of that. Shut her up for good," Dalton said harshly.

"You mean—get rid of her?" Will stared at his brother.

Dalton nodded his head with a jerk.

"No—no, Dalton. We never done nothing like that— not even you! Sure, you held a gun on that man at the grocery store but you didn't shoot him. You were just trying to get him to give up his money. You ain't no murderer and I ain't going to be one either!" Will cried.

"Well, it looks like it's different this time, don't it, brother? 'Cause I'm leaving. I'll be gone from this county, maybe from the whole country. I guess you gotta take care of her however you want." Dalton turned his back on his brother.

Dee sucked in air over the dirty handkerchief. She'd

held her breath so long she felt things turning black around her.

"Can't we go and take her with us? Then we can dump her way down the road," Will begged his brother.

"You got a thick head, Will. I told you. You ain't going with me. And I sure ain't taking her. I just dragged her straight over that mountain and all the way around the lake with my leg paining me all the way."

"Dalton . . ." Will began to beg again.

"Look, you suit yourself what you're going to do. I got to get my stuff together and get over to that car on Koons' place. I can't waste no more time worrying about her, or 'bout you neither." Dalton went into the back room of the old shack.

Will stood kicking at the small rocks covering the ground. His hands were jammed in his pockets. He glanced at Dee under half-closed lids. Then he looked away, dropping his head down.

Will seemed to be thinking very hard. That was probably why Dee heard the sounds first. Her ears picked up the soft sound of brushing weeds by the side of the shed. The next sound was the snap of a clasp, then the harsh panting of breath. David stepped around the corner of the old shack, firmly holding a straining General on his leash. The dog had easily tracked Dalton Snipes. The scattered pepper had actually been a help to General. He could keep his head high right on the scent. He did not have to keep his nose down on a fading ground scent. The strong smell of pepper and the reek of Snipes' tobacco breath and sweaty body marked the trail. The dog had raced over the wooded path.

David removed his pistol from his holster and held it steadily at Will. "Watch him!" David gave the command to his dog. General stood alertly, his front paws planted firmly. His back legs were slightly crouched. He was ready to spring to the attack when commanded.

Stepping around the shed just behind the trooper and his dog, Eric gave a quick look at Will. "You creep! Where is she? What did you do with her?"

Trying to wriggle to move herself better where they could see her, Dee groaned. "Um—um—um!" She bit her teeth against the filthy gag. Her tongue tasted the moldy dirt on it. She was about to be sick.

Eric spotted her movements and started to run toward her. David stayed in position with his gun trained on Will. When Dee saw Eric start toward her, she realized they did not know Dalton Snipes was here! Shaking her head wildly, she tried to warn them. "Uh—uh—uh!"

"I'm coming, Dee! I'll get you untied right now! Just be still!" Eric said as he reached her. He felt behind

her to fumble at the gag. Dee tried to squirm around and let Eric know there was someone else here, too.

"It's okay! It's okay!" Eric said. "I'll get this off. Just be still!" He yanked the gag away from Dee's mouth. She sucked in air, trying to warn them of Dalton Snipes.

Suddenly General's sharp sense of hearing let him know of a new danger. He gave a snarl and almost sprang toward the shed. David held him firmly. "General, no!" The trooper had just seen the arm that suddenly clamped around Eric from the back. David had seen the knife come up against the teenager's throat. He saw Dalton Snipes just as he stepped from the darkness of the shed.

The two Snipes brothers were twenty feet apart. If David went after one or let General attack, there would either be shots or a knife for somebody. The trooper's actions would have to be split in two directions.

Dalton Snipes held his arm tightly across Eric's chest, pinning his arms down. The point of his knife quivered against Eric's throat.

"I wish I had time to jaw with you some, Craven," Dalton Snipes sneered. "It sure was nice of you to drop by for a visit. But I got to be taking a trip. We was just thinking about taking your sister here along." He nudged Dee with the toe of his shoe.

General snarled. His body was quivering with the strain of waiting for his trooper's command to attack.

"Let them both go, Snipes." David's voice was firm and commanding. His pistol was pointing steadily at the older Snipes. His German shepherd tensely waited to spring toward Will or Dalton when the command was given. But that knife was sticking right at Eric's throat. David did not give an attack command.

"Now, I don't believe I can let them go," Dalton drawled. "At least, not both of them. But you'll be happy about this idea of mine. The girl's tied up and I don't aim to carry her like a sack of potatoes. She stays. This boy here is coming with me. You, too, Will. I need you now to help me get him to the car."

Dalton yanked Eric to one side. He jerked his head at Will. "Come on, we're going! If you sic your dog on me, Craven, I'll let him get the boy, not me. Or I'll cut the boy up bad if you make me. So you better not follow us!" he warned.

Walking backwards with Eric as a shield, Dalton and Will started up into the bushes above the lake. Soon they reached the thick shrubs. The bushes closed in after them.

"D—D—David!" Dee turned to her brother.

"Stay!" her brother commanded General. He stooped beside his sister. Quickly, he untied the knots around her feet, then around her hands. She reached up and grabbed his arm. "David, hurry! We have to follow them!"

David pulled her to her feet. "Can you walk? Hurry—loosen up! We have to run if you can make it!" He started pulling her toward the lake. He headed toward the path up around the hill where Dalton Snipes had taken Eric.

Dee stumbled after him. "David, we have to follow them! They're going up the mountain path where he got me. They're going to the barn at—at the Koons' place. That's what Will said!"

"Then they aren't going up the mountain. They will cut down the lower ridge toward the Koons' place. And Will put a stolen car there for Dalton, right?"

"Yes, but how can we find them? They'll be way ahead of us!" Dee was crying. Her face was streaked with dirt. Her mouth was gritty where the gag had been.

David didn't answer her. He was running, dragging her by the hand. He wasn't slowing down any to let her rest. At least he wasn't leaving her back there by herself. General was plunging ahead, racing toward a dirt road curving just beyond the edge of the pasture.

"Did they say anything else? Did you hear where they might be going?" David quickly asked Dee. "Did you hear what kind of car they stole?"

"Uh—uh," Dee gasped. Her legs were shaking. "Texas—Mexico—he was going out of the country, he said. The car—was—was—" She stopped talking.

What had she heard Will say? "I think he said it was a four-door car, that it was cool. That is all he said."

"Okay." David kept her hand firmly in his as he pulled her toward the road. Running on the graveled surface was easier than plunging through the weed-high meadow.

"David, I can't—I . . ." Dee's side was aching fiercely.

"You can't stop. We've come around the base of the mountain. We don't have to go over it. Come on, Dee! My car is at Kelly's house. It's just after the next curve."

Her whole body felt as if it was floating by the time they reached Kelly's house. Dee fell into the front seat of the car, her head drooping down as she tried to slow her racing heart.

"Hup!" David commanded General to jump into the back seat. The husky dog leaped into the back, pacing restlessly on the seat. He was still ready to search, to attack. His job wasn't done yet.

David was in the driver's seat and on his radio to the State Trooper dispatcher in a second. He got information about Dalton Snipes and his break out of the jail. He gave the facts about the stolen car.

"Badge 588." He gave his badge number to the dispatcher. "I believe suspect has left the old Koons place on Route 747 in stolen car. I don't have a license number. Suspect is with his brother, Will Snipes. They have a hostage, Eric Kurtz. Watch your gunfire if suspect is sighted. Suspect is armed with knife. Will Snipes has a rifle. They're heading for the nearest road out of the county from the Koons' place. That should be Route 569. I'm cutting across the mountain on Route 252."

The dispatcher gave an all-out alert for other troopers in the area to aid in hunting the criminal. David kept his radio on but he put his thoughts into pursuit now.

Rocks spewed out from under the wheels of the blue and gray car. David turned on the big flashing light. He flicked the siren on. Dalton Snipes would know they were coming for him. Secrecy would be no help. Speed would.

The blue and gray car tore over the gravel road they had just run along. With the siren screaming a warning, the few cars they met almost went into the ditches to get out of the way. They whizzed past so fast the faces of other drivers were just blurs to Dee.

"D—David, where is Petie? What did you do with him?" she asked.

"He's okay. Don't worry about him. I couldn't search for you with a little boy along. I took him to Eric's mother. That's when Eric came with me to look for you. He's tracked with me before."

"Wh—what will they do with Eric?" Dee asked, her lips chattering.

"Don't worry, Dee. We're going to get them," he said stiffly. "Dalton Snipes thinks he's the only one who knows the back roads in this county. I know them every bit as good now as he does. He'll be on the road following the ridge of Spruce Mountain. I'll lay a bet on that. It's the only one not traveled much that still leads him to the state line. He'll think I don't know about it but this is my county now. And I know it as well as he does. Hang on!" David suddenly warned as he spun the patrol car sharply to the right onto a dirt road. The motor roared as David shifted gears to begin the climb up the ridge.

Dee hung on to the side, her safety belt cutting across her shoulder. They twisted and turned in hairpin curves as they sped steadily up. Dee's ears began to feel tight as the car gained altitude.

"David, could he have taken another road?" Dee asked. She was frightened as curve after curve came up and there was no sign of a four-door car. There was no sign of *any* car until they swung around a laurel-covered hill. A small black pickup was tilted into a ditch hugging the mountain. David skidded to a quick stop. He yelled to the driver, "Are you hurt? Is anybody hurt?"

"No! But dang it!" A farmer sat with his hands on the wheel. "That dern fool who just passed me, he came tearing around that curve like he was in the Indy

500. If I hadn't put myself in this ditch, he would have hit me straight! Or else he would have gone roaring off into that valley down there." He pointed to the sharp drop on David's side of the road. "You fellows ought to keep people like that off the road!"

"Yes, sir. That's just what I'm going to do. What color was the car, please, sir? Could you tell the make? The license number?" David quickly asked.

"Color? Yes, kind of a wheat color," the elderly man said.

"Would you say cream?" David asked.

"Yeah, that's good. It was a color like cream. I don't know the make," the farmer said. "I didn't have time to see the license number he was gone so dern fast. But there was more than one of them in there. Just out to have a good time like some of these kids today. They don't have respect like they used to!"

David broke in. "I'll radio for help for you. I have to stay on the tail of that car."

The farmer's eyes widened. "Is that right? He's done something bad? Well, well!"

The trooper's car sped up and around the curve. David braked quickly and was around another curve. They climbed steadily to the top of the ridge where the road smoothed out.

David increased his speed as long as they were driving along this easier stretch. When they started down the mountain, he shifted the gears lower to help hold the car. The next curve showed a cloud of dust settling back down to the road in front of them.

"We've got him," David said grimly.

Dee just hung on as the tires screeched around still another curve. Then she yelled, "There he is, David!" She pointed to the back of the cream-colored car disappearing around still another curve.

David's car siren was still going. The circular light on top flashed its warning. But Dalton Snipes didn't slow down at all. He swerved the cream-colored car into the middle of the road. David could not pull up beside him even if the road had been wide enough.

The bumper of the trooper's car was just feet away from the back of the stolen car. There was so much dust it was not possible to see how many people were in the car.

David gripped the steering wheel with one hand like steel. He used his other hand to lift his mike and give an update to the dispatcher. "I have suspect in sight, traveling west on Route 252. I have just passed the peak of Spruce Mountain. I'm on the downgrade . . ." He paused.

The cream-colored car in front swerved wildly around a curve that hooked sharply back to the left. The stolen car began to fishtail over the sliding gravel. The right wheels dipped down off the road. The car tilted farther as it crashed into the dusty bushes edging the steep bank.

Dee's hands went up to her mouth. The cream car flipped over once. It struck a stand of stalk-thin trees, snapping them off as it rolled again.

David eased down on his brakes. With lights still flashing, the trooper's car came to a stop. David spoke into his mike. "Badge 588. Request ambulance and trooper assistance on State Road 252. I'm three miles north from the top of Spruce Mountain." He paused as he watched the door on the driver's side of the cream car. It suddenly opened up as it lay on its side. Dalton Snipes crawled out, shaking his head. He didn't even look back into the stolen car. He stared quickly up the slope to the trooper's car with its flashing light. Then, limping, he began to tear off down the ridge.

David started talking rapidly into the mike. "Also, request for helicopter assistance for capture of suspect."

He jumped from the patrol car. General whined to share in the hunt. Dee scrambled out of her seat. Tearing through the thick mountain laurel, they scrambled to find Eric.

"Please let Eric be okay. Please let him be alive!" Dee's thoughts tumbled over and over.

10

Scrambling through the brush, David and Dee came up behind the wrecked car. With a hand held up to warn Dee, the trooper stopped. He pointed to a big tree with a silent order for Dee to hide there. He un-snapped his holster and drew out his gun. Releasing the safety, he pointed the gun straight up. Then he cautiously approached the car.

There was a hissing sound as steam spewed out from the broken radiator. The front end was crushed against big rocks protruding from the bushes. The windshield was cracked and splintered. Carefully, David eased his way up to the car. Dee watched as her brother peered down into the car resting on its side. Then, very quickly, he slipped his pistol back into the holster.

"Quick, Dee, there's a first aid kit in my car. Get it!" he called to his sister.

She pushed her way toward him through the bushes. "Is it Eric? He's hurt, isn't he?"

David shook his head. "It's Will. He's really hurt. Eric isn't here."

"Not there! But they had him! Maybe—maybe he's under the car . . . David!" Her voice was rising.

"Dee, straighten up! Eric is not here! Either they dumped . . . either they let him go earlier or Dalton Snipes took him from the car. Maybe we just didn't see him. But he's not here! Now, hurry, Dee. Will looks bad. Get my kit!" he ordered.

The stern tone of his voice made her calm down. She began to claw her way back up the side of the ravine. David quickly called after her. "Dee! Go up to the car easy. General is pretty keyed up. Be sure he knows who you are before you reach for the keys. The first aid kit is in the trunk."

Dee reached the road and moved toward the car. General was pacing the back seat excitedly. As she came up to the car, Dee began talking to him. "Hi, General! It's me. You know me. It's Dee."

The dog stood alertly. The hair on the back of his neck was standing up. Slowly Dee started to put her hand in the front window to get the keys. The German shepherd bared his teeth. His snarl made Dee snatch her hand back.

"Ohh—General, stop it!" The dog's eyes gleamed as he continued to guard his car for his trooper. His excitement had grown so intense he would let no one else, not even Dee, near his car.

"General! I've got to get that kit! David told me to!" General was not ready to cooperate. His job was to guard his car against anyone except David.

Dee stepped back from the car. She dropped her hands down by her sides. When she heard a car roaring up the mountain road, she stepped out of the way behind the patrol car.

Another blue and gray Virginia State Police car pulled up right in front of David's. Just before the driver hopped out, Dee heard the trooper reporting arrival on the service radio. "I'm 10-23 on the scene of wreck near the top of Spruce Mountain." Quickly, the driver stepped from the patrol car. Spotting Dee, the trooper asked curtly, "Where is Sergeant Craven?"

Dee stared at the first woman trooper she had seen out on the road. The trooper's dark hair was swirled up in a neat bun and held by a wide clasp. She looked younger than David.

"Miss—I asked you. Where is Trooper Craven? He radioed for assistance. I picked it up on my beeper when I was in line in the grocery store."

"He's down there!" Dee pointed.

The young woman turned quickly to go down the ravine. David could be seen leaning inside the wrecked car.

"Wait!" Dee said. "General won't let me get the keys.

I can't get to the first aid kit. Do you have one? David needs it in a hurry!"

"Of course, I have one," the young woman answered. She reached back in her car. Getting her kit, she started down to assist David.

Dee watched from the road. She knew she couldn't help. When the noise of an ambulance siren reached them, David came back up the steep bank. He had been the first trooper on the scene. That put him in charge of all operations. He directed the rescue workers down to the crushed car.

David did not go back down. He sat in his car, door open, as he set up plans over the service radio with the dispatcher.

"Badge 288. We have one suspect under rescue care. He is badly injured. Ambulance will transport as soon as possible. Badge 129 is on the scene to help. I request helicopter assistance in tracking main suspect. Main suspect has escaped into woods off Route 252. Uncertain whether main suspect still has hostage with him. Alert troopers aiding in search to check area spreading from crest of ridge down to riverbank. It is believed suspect now has gun and knife. Request troopers search from Koons' place to this point for sign of hostage."

"10-4, Badge 588. Helicopter is approaching your location. Go on TAC channel now for direct radio contact to inform pilot of best landing area."

"10-4," David answered briskly.

Switching his radio to contact the chopper himself, David was soon talking with the pilot. Even before the change in the sound of the voice over the radio, Dee knew the pilot was Eric's father. Sergeant Kurtz asked for no personal information. He had to put business first. But David gave all details to the pilot.

"Badge 588. I have visual contact of you, 315," David said as the helicopter appeared over the topmost ridge. It hovered just above the treetops while David and Sergeant Kurtz set up plans. David brought the pilot up to date.

"One suspect is injured. The rescue squad is preparing him for transport to hospital. The main suspect has escaped. He was heading down the mountain toward the river when last seen. I need your help in tracking him. I'm preparing to start out with General now," David said. Then he added in a quieter tone, "Third person who was being held hostage is not in the car. There is no sign of the hostage at this time."

For just a minute there was no comment from the helicopter pilot. Then Sergeant Kurtz asked, "Has dispatcher been alerted to request trooper assistance in locating hostage?"

"10-4. That request has already been made. They'll find Eric." David broke his usual businesslike tone. The pilot was his best friend, the son was like a younger brother. Eric had to be found.

Again the helicopter pilot was silent for a moment. Finally, there came a muffled, "Thanks." Then the pilot came back on strongly. "I've spotted a brick building with a level grassy area. It's about one and a half miles from you. I can set down there. Dee's with you, isn't she? She can go with me for an extra pair of eyes. She's seen more of the main suspect than I have. She'll be a big help, okay?"

David agreed with that. He knew Dee could really help to spot Dalton Snipes. And in this wooded area they were going to need all the help they could get. It was already dusk. They would need sharp eyes to spot Dalton Snipes. Also, General's nose would be more valuable than ever as it grew darker. David knew it was going to be all he could do to handle General as he was tracking Dalton Snipes. The trooper could expect to be dragged through the woods by this 100-pound dog eagerly tracking the criminal. He would need those extra eyes from Dee and from the helicopter pilot to help in the search.

"Dee!" David turned to her quickly as he replaced his mike. "Get down the road just below here. Kurtz is setting down to take you on board."

"Me! Why? I've never been in a helicopter! Where is he taking me?"

Hurriedly, David pulled his armor jacket on over his uniform. Then he began getting General ready to search.

"Hup!" he commanded and General jumped out the open door. Eagerly, he waited for the trooper to get started. First, David gave General some of the fresh water he carried along for his dog. Then he allowed the dog to go to the bathroom. Only then did he start to get the dog keyed up and excited for the search.

"Do you want to find it? General, let's get to work! Let's find it!"

When Dee spoke again, he looked up, startled. His attention had been totally on his dog.

"David, what good could I be in that helicopter?" the girl asked. Her voice was trembling.

"Dee, hurry! Every minute lost is that much farther Snipes can get away. The chopper has already landed down there! Hurry! Kurtz is waiting for you. He needs your eyes to help search!"

Dee started running down the road. Behind her in the early evening dusk shone the red lights from the ambulance. The lights from the two Virginia State Police cars whirled around and around. Her feet stumbled over the pebbles in the road. Dee ran along muttering, "Oh, gosh—oh, gosh!"

When she turned the bend, she saw the helicopter settled onto the grassy area beside the building. She had to make herself keep on running toward it. Sergeant Kurtz was standing beside the chopper. He was still in contact with David through the TAC channel.

Ducking her head under the whirling blades, Dee hurried up to the open helicopter door.

Instantly, Sergeant Kurtz climbed in, too, and started the engine up faster. He motioned for Dee to fasten her seat belt. Suddenly they were swooping straight up and then dipping sideways down over the ridges below. Dee's stomach swooped right along with the motion. She squeezed her eyes shut and clenched her hands on her knees.

"Easy, Dee," Sergeant Kurtz's voice came to her. "You've flown before. You'll get used to it. Open your eyes but don't look down. Look straight ahead at something. And don't hold your breath. Take deep breaths!"

For an answer Dee grabbed the motion sickness bag between their seats and promptly lost her lunch. The pilot didn't say a word. Dee was so embarrassed she almost cried. She wiped her face on the clean cloth he held out to her.

"Better?" he asked over the roar of the helicopter engine. Dee nodded, ashamed she was so chicken. The pilot said, "Hey, don't feel so bad. A lot of people have trouble getting used to the motion of a helicopter. It's up, it's down, it goes like a big swing to one side and then the other."

Dee's eyes opened wide in alarm. He'd better stop describing these wavy movements. He'd better stop or she was going to barf again!

"Hey, I'm sorry!" he said when he saw the look on her face. "I thought you were over it. Just pick one spot to keep your eyes on. Then you won't get so dizzy."

Dee tried. Her face and hands felt clammy but the cool mountain air coming in began to help. She leaned her head back and took some big deep breaths.

"Are you okay?" Sergeant Kurtz asked as he reached for the mike. He waited for Dee's answer before he began to make contact with David on the ground. Dee nodded. Her face was beginning to get some color back.

"Badge 315. We're 10-17 now. Which direction do you want us to head? Do you have a track yet?" Kurtz asked for David's orders.

"Do you have Dee? How's she doing?" David asked first.

The pilot looked over at Dee. He grinned and said, "She can barf with the best of them!"

"She's sick! Why? She's flown before."

"You forget. Helicopter flying is different from fixed-wing craft flying. Besides, she's had a rough day, don't you think? She'll do fine. She's a real trooper," the pilot answered. "Right, Dee?"

Dee nodded. She sat up straighter and began looking down over the treetops they were skimming. Oh, gosh. She looked back up to the sky. That wasn't so good either!

David's voice crackled over the mike with his order to the pilot. "Go straight down from this ridge. Snipes was heading that way. He's got a good start on us but I think his leg is hurting so that may slow him down. Give him a mile straight down and then start a grid pattern. Maybe if he is there and sees you doing that, it will at least contain him in that area. I'll be tracking with General from this point. I'm going to start General with the wagon-wheel pattern. When he gets the scent, I'll give you the exact direction."

"It's going to be dark soon," Kurtz said. "I hope he decides to go more in the open or we'll have trouble spotting him."

"Maybe not," David answered. "You have your eyes and your search light. I have General's nose. They are both the best things we have going for us."

"And me," Dee spoke up.

"Hey," the pilot said to David, "she spoke! She's back with us, I think. Craven, if you find out anything about the hostage—let me know." Tension crept into his voice. He was first of all a pilot with a safe flight his main work. His second work was as a police officer. But he was also the father of the hostage. He could keep that worry under tight control, but he could not forget it.

David answered, "10-4. You, too. You let me know."

They started in on the trail of Dalton Snipes. From

the helicopter the strong glare of the searchlight bore into the growing darkness of the trees on the ground. Briefly, Dee looked up to see how the pilot was flying and still working the bright light. The beam hit tree after tree. It picked up dark shadows near rocks. None of them turned out to be Dalton Snipes.

"What was he wearing, Dee?" Sergeant Kurtz asked.

"He had on an old blue jacket and khaki pants, dirty ones," she answered.

"Um, that's going to be hard to spot in this dark. He'll fade right into the landscape."

"We've got to find him! Maybe—maybe he still has Eric with him. That would be easier to spot. Eric had on a white T-shirt and jeans," she said.

Sergeant Kurtz didn't answer. Suddenly there came an interruption. David was making contact with them again.

"Badge 588. I'm now about one mile down the ridge. General has been tracking strongly up until now. But he's acting very strange. He may be losing the trail."

"What is he doing?" Sergeant Kurtz asked David.

"He tracks straight for awhile. Then all of a sudden he makes a complete circle around a tree. Then he tracks straight again and around in a circle once more. He's been doing this for about fifty feet. I honestly don't know what his problem is."

"I do!" the pilot responded. "He's on a good track.

I've known this to happen before when I was using my searchlight in a wooded area. Snipes is stopping behind a tree every time I swing over him and he's circling that tree to keep out of my beam. So General is circling right on Snipes' scent. He's doing great!"

"Good boy! Good dog, General!" They heard David praise the dog. Then David said, "Now, come on. Find him!"

The helicopter and the ground trackers bore in as swiftly as they could on the fresh scent being left by Dalton Snipes. The suspect seemed to be heading for the riverbank at the base of the mountain.

The helicopter swooped up on an old summer cottage near the river. Its searchlight probed down into the dark. The glare picked at each shadow. Nothing moved in the flood of light. As the pilot moved the helicopter into a swooping turn, Dee looked back down on the front steps of the old house. She saw something move at the edge.

"Something's there!" Dee whispered. She was terrified as she remembered the filthy smell of Dalton Snipes. "I think it's him! He's at that house! I think I saw him!"

"You spotted him?" the pilot asked alertly. "Is he alone? Does he have the hostage with him?"

"I don't know," Dee said tensely. "I could only see something. It looked like that—that man."

Quickly, the pilot reached for his mike. "Badge 315. Suspect may have been spotted. As you come toward the riverbank, something has been spotted moving near the front of that old house. We'll keep him contained until you reach the site. We will not try to set down and capture. We will wait until you reach the site to assist. You must be almost to the river."

David's voice came back excitedly. "General's on the scent strong! We must be close. He's almost pulling me off my feet. Don't let Snipes get away! Keep him pinned down. Fire if you have to."

"Right! We'll keep the searchlight pinned on that house. I'll fire near him if necessary to hold him there."

The helicopter chattered busily over the darkened house. It looked in very run-down shape. It did not appear to be used by anyone anymore. There was no further sign of Dalton Snipes. Dee began to wonder if she really had seen him. And if he was there, was Eric there, too?

"I'm closing in," David's voice came suddenly over the radio. "Set down when you see me approaching that house. Give me backup as soon as you can. Dalton Snipes is armed. I'm going in with General now." The sound of his voice stopped abruptly.

11

The darkness of night had closed over the hills, spreading into each ravine and finally over every ridge. It was not possible to see David and General. The bright searchlight zoomed in on the old house backing up against the trees. Unless there was a way Dalton Snipes could break in and get through that house to the back, he was cornered.

Sergeant Kurtz kept the brilliant light pinned right on the front of the house. Slowly he maneuvered the helicopter down onto the level ground by the river. The blades spun to a slow stop. As the sound of the engine cut off, the pilot reached for his pistol. With the front of the house pinpointed in the glaring spotlight, he would have a perfect sight on the suspect.

Suddenly there was a movement in the bushes.

Straining at his leash, General clawed his way into the clearing. David was leaning back to keep the dog under control. Slowly, David let the dog move ahead. General was close on the track of Dalton Snipes.

The trooper and his dog crept toward the floodlit house. Dee could see them moving along the dark edge of the lighted area. Sergeant Kurtz stayed alertly in the pilot's seat. His gun was trained on the sagging door of the old house.

Suddenly the dog stopped. He lifted his head to the wind and sniffed. Over the sounds of the night, Dee could hear the dog whine. David watched the dog but he gave no new command to General. The dog turned his head to the right. His nose pointed toward the dark woods at the back of the house. Then he windscented back to the front. It was clear that Dalton Snipes was on the move again! Had he crawled out through the house somehow? There was no way to see. The old house looked so rotten he might have crawled through a hole.

David suddenly dropped to a crouch. "Down, General! Crawl!" The whispered command carried on the wind to the helicopter. The pilot had his door open. He was ready to assist Trooper Craven and the dog.

David and General kept in the shadows. They inched their way around the edge of the house. Dee watched, peeping through her hands held over her eyes. When David reached the edge of the house, he stayed close to the side. Slowly, he began to creep around the corner.

Suddenly General gave a different alert. He swirled to snarl at the porch jutting out from the side of the house. David trusted his dog's abilities. He signaled to the helicopter pilot to shift the position of the searchlight. At once, Sergeant Kurtz swung the light to cover as much of the porch as possible. When the glare hit that edge, a shot pinged against the side of the helicopter.

"Down!" the pilot yelled at Dee. She ducked farther down into her seat. Covering her eyes all the way, she only heard the pilot. He had jumped from the helicopter. His feet thudded on the ground. She heard his steps running away from the helicopter.

He had left her here by herself, Dee thought! Very slowly, she peeped over the lower edge of the window. Sergeant Kurtz was just slipping into the shadows behind the house. He would quickly be in a position to cover the back porch. Dalton Snipes would not find an easy escape.

No more shots came toward the helicopter. The light still shone brightly on the edge of the house. Dee felt as if she were in a theater watching a play in the glare of footlights. A pretend play would have been much easier to take. This was no make-believe scene. This stage was for real.

Her knees were quivering. Her hands were sweating. Watching the silent scene in the glare of the light, Dee felt as if she couldn't get enough air to breathe.

Suddenly everything in front of her exploded into action! There came the sudden sound of wood splintering and Dalton Snipes crashed his way through the rotting side boards of the back porch. He fired straight at the trooper and his dog as they started up the center steps. When a shot zinged at him from the trees, Snipes whirled and fired his rifle toward the dark woods behind the house.

With a zigzagging run, Dalton Snipes sped toward the helicopter. And right in front of her view, Dee saw how a search dog is also an attack dog. She heard David's sharp command. "Get him, General!"

David had dropped the leash and the dog now pounded across the dirt toward Dalton Snipes. His paws tore into the dirt as he sprang for the suspect, knocking him to the ground. The dog tore at the suspect's shirt. Snipes was twisting and turning under the dog's attack.

"Out!" David shouted his command as Snipes lay on the ground. Instantly, General pulled back from the man lying on the ground.

"Watch him!" came David's next command as he ran toward his dog and the suspect. On the ground Dalton Snipes lay with his face in the dirt. He didn't move until David was near him. Then he turned his

head. He looked up at the trooper with a hatred that strained at his face.

His anger made him careless. He swirled on the dirt and lunged for David's leg. General waited for no command. The dog was trained to attack again if needed. He was trained to protect his trooper at all costs. This was what the dog lived for. And Dalton Snipes had just made a very stupid move. This time the dog leaped across the ground. He didn't grab for clothing. He sank his teeth into Snipes' arm.

The criminal screamed and hit at the dog with his free hand. General never let go. His snarls were as loud as Dalton Snipes' screams.

With his gun aimed down at the struggling pair on the ground, David finally commanded, "Out!" General did not want to let go this time. Firmly, David gave the command again. "Out, General! Out!"

From the helicopter Dee could see that General did not want to let the prisoner go. But he followed his trooper's order. He released Snipes' arm. He didn't move away. He stood over the man on the ground. The dog was just begging for a chance to sink his teeth into the man one more time.

Dalton Snipes wasn't totally stupid. He didn't try anything again. With General's teeth bared and David's gun trained on him, he turned his face away and into the dirt. His blue denim jacket was torn and bloody.

When Sergeant Kurtz ran up, Snipes just lay there while the pilot yanked the prisoner's hands behind his back and locked shackles on them. He wasn't very gentle as he hustled Snipes to stand up. When Snipes moved his feet to get his balance, General was crouched ready to spring at him again.

With his gun still trained on Snipes, David abruptly asked him, "Where's the boy? Where's Eric?"

Dee held her breath, waiting for the prisoner's answer. There was none. This was Snipes' only chance to get back at David. He wanted David to beg for an answer Snipes wasn't going to give him.

David said sternly again, "Where is he, Snipes?"

Dalton Snipes just stood there and stared at the trooper. He smirked as the question stayed unanswered.

David took a step toward Snipes. General was ready to take a leap. His gleaming eyes had never left Snipes. He was just waiting for any reason to attack.

Sergeant Kurtz touched David's shoulder. "Hold off. He's just trying to get at us. We'll find Eric."

David muttered, "You creep!" He kept on staring at Snipes. "You are a filthy excuse for a human being. If you've hurt that boy . . ." He stopped. Then he went on, "The charge will be kidnapping this time, Snipes. Two counts on you! My sister and Eric Kurtz. Your sentence for robbery was nothing to what you'll get now. I'll see to that! And you'll have another charge—contributing to the delinquency of a minor. Maybe we can get your brother straightened out—*if* he recovers from his injuries." David was quivering from the disgust and anger he felt toward Dalton Snipes.

Sergeant Kurtz said, "I'll radio for someone to come get Dee. Then we'll take Snipes back to jail."

"Right," David said. He aimed his gun steadily at Snipes. "And General and I will go with you to transport him."

Snipes was hauled into the helicopter. His feet were chained. Guarded by both trooper and dog, Snipes would have no chance of escape.

Another Virginia trooper soon appeared in his blue and gray car. Dee was glad it wasn't anyone she knew. She was wiped out. If he began to ask her about the capture, she couldn't talk. She just couldn't.

The trooper did not leave the area until the helicopter was airborne. Dee watched from the patrol car until the chopper lifted up and over the trees. The trooper on the ground then contacted the dispatcher on his service radio. "Badge 133. I'm 10-24 on this scene. I'm en route to take kidnap victim to her location. Do you have further traffic for me?"

"Negative," the dispatcher answered.

When the trooper got Dee to the Kurtz house by the lake, Dee said only one thing to Eric's mother. Mrs.

Kurtz had come quickly out of the house to the car. Dee looked at her.

"Eric?" the teenager asked Mrs. Kurtz.

"I've been listening to the scanner. They haven't found him yet," Mrs. Kurtz said in a worried tone. She looked quickly at the trooper. He shook his head. Mrs. Kurtz quietly said to Dee, "No—nothing yet."

Dee rubbed at her eyes. Where was Eric? She was so tired. She was so tired of being scared. What had happened to him?

"Come with me, Dee. You need some rest. Come on now." Mrs. Kurtz led her into the house.

"I'll fix you something hot to eat. Go on now. Go in my bathroom and take a long hot shower. There are some jeans and shirts Eric's sister left the last time she was home. I put them on the bathroom rack for you. I think they'll fit. Go on now, Dee." She gave the girl a little push toward the bathroom.

Dee let the hot water wash and wash and wash away the dirt. It would be awhile before anything could clean away the filth she felt from Dalton Snipes.

Delicious smells drifted out from the kitchen. Dee was too tired to care. While she was sitting on Mrs. Kurtz's bed drying her hair with a towel, she leaned back for just a minute. She stared at the picture on the low pine chest. Sergeant Kurtz was pictured with two other pilots. They knelt in front of the Virginia

State Police helicopter and fixed-wing plane they flew.

Mrs. Kurtz looked in the door. "Dee, come on now. You need something to eat."

The girl shook her head. She couldn't eat. "Mrs. Kurtz, is it okay if I go down by the lake—for just awhile?"

Mrs. Kurtz nodded slowly. "Go ahead. That will be good for you, Dee. Just lie on the dock awhile. This food will keep. You do whatever makes you feel better."

Dee slowly stood up. Everything ached. When she went out the kitchen door, Mrs. Kurtz pretended to be very busy at the sink.

Following the path down to the lake, Dee never looked up. She thought her shaking legs weren't going to even get her there. She finally reached the little dock. Huddled on the rough boards, Dee felt the warmth from the early morning sun just seep into her.

"Go away—go away, everything!" she murmured. Tears stayed behind her closed eyelids. And finally she could sleep.

It was late morning when Dee finally opened her eyes. Something had touched her arm. She sat up suddenly, making her head swim.

"Hey, I didn't mean to scare you," Eric said. His smile was a little lopsided. He had a huge bruise on one cheek. There was a wide bandage on his forehead.

"Eric—you—you're here—I mean you're okay!" Dee's

154

eyes flooded and she covered her face. She was embarrassed for showing how she felt.

"Well, I know I look ugly but you don't have to cover your eyes! You look a mess yourself," he said, ruffling her hair. He was trying to get her to laugh.

"I know that," Dee said. She tried to straighten her borrowed clothes. "But look at your face! And your head!"

"It's okay. I've been to the hospital for an X-ray. I've had a shower. And you've been asleep all this time!"

"What happened to you?" Dee asked, starting to touch his bandaged forehead.

"Ouch on that!" Eric said, taking her hand away from his face. He held her hand instead. "Dalton Snipes gave me a good whack on the head when they got to that stolen car. Will had hidden it at the old Koons' place. I guess Dalton thought I'd be extra baggage instead of a help so he dumped me there. That's where one of the troopers found me, somewhere near there. I don't remember." He gave her hand a squeeze. "I hear you had a rough time. I'm sorry."

Dee's voice shook. "I was so scared. I was scared of everything, even with your dad in the helicopter."

Eric chuckled at that. "Yeah, I hear you can barf with the best of them!"

"Well, I couldn't help that!" Dee felt her face grow hot.

"Look, some people would pass out with all you went through. I guess the troopers all think you were super. And I hear that you were the one who first spotted Dalton Snipes at that old house. From what they have said, I'd like to have you on my side anytime."

Dee stared down at the dock. She was too surprised to say anything. Eric squeezed her hand again.

"Is that okay, Dee? I mean it. Do you want to stay by my side? We can maybe learn how to face a lot of things—together."

"I . . . I think I could try harder if . . . if we try together." Dee held onto Eric's hand.

"Then that's settled," Eric said. "And being together right now means eating together. I think Mom cooks a lot when she gets worried! The oven looks full. Are you ready for something?"

"I can handle that!" Dee grinned.

"Well, come on!" He pulled her to her feet. "If we help each other, maybe we can make it back up this hill, even with our aches and pains!"

RUTH HALLMAN is the author of *Panic Five, Midnight Wheels, Rescue Chopper, Breakaway, Tough Is Not Enough,* and other stories popular with teenage readers. Her years of teaching experience and her work with young people in hospitals and detention homes are reflected in her books. All are exciting, dramatic adventures written in an easy-to-read style.

Mrs. Hallman is also the author of teacher/student textbook materials. She maintains her awareness of the current interests of readers by giving writing presentations and workshops to schools, libraries, teacher and librarian organizations.

Ruth Hallman lives in Virginia with her husband, Bob, where she is a Research Associate at Virginia Polytechnic Institute. Their two daughters, one in high school, one in college, and their two sons, both college graduates, have always been a source of valuable inspiration and information for her writing.